"How many other pieces of land has he ruined?"

"None!" Luke said.

"As far as you know," Carly replied.

He shook his head in frustration. "I can't answer that, or give you any facts that I don't have."

"Luke, from what you've said so far, you wouldn't tell me even if you did know."

Before he could answer, she threw her hands in the air. "Never mind. This is a pointless...merry-go-round. Nightmare-go-round," she amended. "It's time for you to go, Luke, and...and don't come back."

"Carly, if you'd listen to me, I can at least tell you—"

"Lies?" She held up her hand. "No. Go."

As if to emphasize her fury, the windows rattled in their frames.

"Earthquake," she said accusingly.

"Well, I didn't cause it."

"Yet."

Luke swung toward the door. "I'll be back in three months, Carly, and I hope you'll have to listen to me."

"Don't count on it."

Dear Reader,

Welcome back to Reston, Oklahoma. I hope you enjoyed your visit to the southeastern part of the state in *At Odds with the Midwife*. *The Husband She Can't Forget* is the story of Carly Joslin and Luke Sanderson, who married much too young and parted painfully years ago. Now Luke is back and will be starting an oil-extraction process near Joslin Gardens, where Carly grows organic fruits and vegetables. His process could threaten her livelihood and her land itself. Worst of all, his presence is bringing back memories and regrets she's tried to forget. Having him around will make her face the past even as Luke attempts to succeed in his new venture and avoid hurting Carly again.

Happy reading,

Patricia

HEARTWARMING

The Husband She Can't Forget

USA TODAY Bestselling Author

Patricia Forsythe

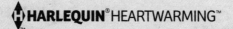

Recycling programs
for this product may
not exist in your area.

ISBN-13: 978-0-373-36824-2

The Husband She Can't Forget

Printed in U.S.A.

Patricia Forsythe is the author of many romance novels and is proud to have received her twenty-five-book pin from Harlequin. She hopes there are many more books to come. A native Arizonan, Patricia loves setting books in areas where she has spent time, like the beautiful Kiamichi Mountains of Oklahoma. She has held a number of jobs, including teaching school, working as a librarian and as a secretary, and operating a care home for developmentally disabled children. Her favorite occupation, though, is writing novels in which the characters get into challenging situations and then work their way out. Each situation and set of characters is different, so sometimes the finished book is as much of a surprise to her as it is to the readers.

Books by Patricia Forsythe

Harlequin Heartwarming

Oklahoma Girls

At Odds with the Midwife

Her Lone Cowboy

Visit the Author Profile page
at Harlequin.com for more titles.

This book is dedicated to my beautiful grandchildren, who give me hope and happiness.

CHAPTER ONE

THE CRUNCH OF tires as a pickup turned onto the long, graveled drive of Joslin Gardens caused a bobwhite quail to cease the endless reciting of his name and brought Carly Joslin's attention from the damp, woven cloth she was spreading over the truck bed of fresh-picked vegetables. She frowned. She didn't recognize the silver dual-cab pickup and she was running short on time. She had to deliver this load of produce to a restaurant on the other side of the county and then change clothes for the Memorial Day barbecue, where she hoped to arrive on time.

It couldn't be a customer. The fresh produce stand that a couple of high school kids operated for her was shuttered for the day and her employees had gone home. However, people did tend to stop by to ask her advice on gardening, or to purchase one of the pieces of furniture she refurbished. Raising a hand to shade her eyes, she tried to peer through the truck's tinted windshield to identify her visitor. She usually enjoyed visits from her customers, but there really wasn't time for an extended chat with anyone today, and besides…

Shock jolted through her, nearly buckling her knees, when she recognized the driver.

"It can't be," she whispered as she felt color drain from her face. "What's he doing here?"

Shakily, she gripped the side of the truck while she reminded herself to breathe and forced her frozen expression into what she hoped was an approximation of a welcoming smile.

The fancy pickup took the rutted and pocked drive slowly, probably to minimize gravel popping up and marring the perfect paint job. The recent rains had laid waste to the drive and Carly intended to have it graded and graveled as soon as the weather improved for an extended period. Now, however, she was glad she had waited. The longer it took for the vehicle to reach her, the more time she had to prepare herself to meet the driver.

Still, she couldn't quite resist the urge to compare the upscale vehicle with her own truck, which her father had bought the year she was born and everyone in the family had used since then. The only thing new was its paint job: dark green with the Joslin Gardens logo she'd created on the sides—curling vines and plump vegetables shaped like letters and numbers. Her pickup ran beautifully except for the air-conditioning, which no one could coax into doing its job.

The silver truck stopped several feet away from her and Luke Sanderson stepped out of the cab. Instantly she saw that he wasn't the gangly boy she'd known a dozen years ago, but a self-assured man dressed in crisp jeans and a dark purple shirt.

He was taller than she remembered, but that might be due to his cowboy boots. When she'd known him before, he'd usually worn work boots, sneakers or sandals. The blond hair that had once hung shaggily around his ears was now perfectly cut. It appeared to be a shade darker, and his skin less tanned, probably because he'd spent the intervening years in an office, not working outside as he had back then.

There was no sign of the beard he'd once

had. Instead his jaw was smooth shaven. His face was fuller. One thing hadn't changed, though. His eyes were still a light shade of caramel brown that had so intrigued her from the minute they'd met.

"Hello, Carly," he said, shutting the pickup's door behind him and walking over to stand in front of her.

His voice was deeper, she thought, but maybe that was because she hadn't heard it in so many years. For some crazy reason, her pounding heart had bounced into her throat.

"Hello, Lu-Luke," she stammered, pausing and trying to get a grip on her emotions. This was the first time she'd spoken to him in twelve years. "This is a surprise."

"I should have called, but it seemed easier to drop by." He nodded toward his truck. "I've got something for you. I thought if you weren't here, I could leave it on the porch with a note."

"Something for me?" She lifted her hands, palm out, as she shook her head. "After all these years, Luke, I can't imagine..."

"It's from Wendolin."

"Your grandmother? But she's—"

"She left you this in her will. Left it to both of us, actually, but it's not something I'd be interested in, so it's all yours."

"What is it?"

"Come on. I'll show you." He walked to the back of the pickup, opened the tailgate and untied the ropes firmly holding a tarp in place around a big, rectangular object.

Although her knees felt a little shaky, Carly followed him. When he flipped the tarp to one side, she gasped.

"Wendolin's hope chest," she breathed, tears filling her eyes. Reaching out a shaky hand, she ran her fingers over the ornately carved flat top of the trunk. "This is the one that was in her bedroom, isn't it? At the foot of her bed."

"Yes." Luke's throat worked and he cleared it before he went on. "She designated years ago that you were to have it. She said you would appreciate it more than anyone else because you love things with a history."

"That's true. I…I do appreciate it. And she left this to me? I never expected her to do such a thing."

"She always loved you. Your visits to her these past few years meant a lot."

"They meant a lot to me, too, but certainly didn't mean she had to leave me a family heirloom." Tears stung her eyes and Carly blinked them back.

"It did to her…and to me."

Carly couldn't form an answer around the knot of sorrow, longing and regret that clogged her throat. Wendolin Bayer had been a wonderful, loving woman, a steadfast friend when Carly had needed one the most.

"My dad…"

"What about him?" Carly choked out. Turning away, she used the sleeve of her T-shirt to dab at her eyes. Robert Sanderson was the last person in the world she wanted to talk about, or even think about, right now.

"He said he saw you at Omi's funeral," he said.

"Along with about six hundred other people. Between her church work and her community work, many people loved her. It was the most crowded funeral I've ever seen." Carly faced him again, her eyes still bright with tears.

"I didn't see you."

"Were you looking for me?" She didn't know what point he was trying to make, and maybe he didn't, either. She had seen him at the funeral, from a distance, but had avoided him. She couldn't face talking to him, and she definitely hadn't wanted to talk to his father. She had made it a point to slip in as the service started and sit in the back, one of the few seats left, and grieve on her own.

When Luke didn't respond, she went on. "I only stayed for the service then I came home. I had produce to pick and deliver."

Luke glanced around, seeming to notice the gardens for the first time, along with the loaded bed of the pickup. His attention lingered on the greenhouses, then on the rows of carrots and beets in the small field. "This is beautiful, Carly. Prosperous. Do you have any help?"

"Some. Mostly high school kids who may or may not be dependable. If I need to, I can manage on my own."

Eager to be finished with this awkward encounter, she reached out, ready to pull the trunk toward her, but Luke put a restraining hand on her arm. She jerked away then blushed when she caught the dismay in his face.

"Sorry," he said. "But it's heavy, so I'd better get it. Omi left a bunch of things in there for you. I didn't look at the contents, thought it was none of my business."

"I can do it." Carly flexed her biceps. "I do manual labor all day long. I can help you with this trunk."

Luke looked at her arm then at her determined face. "Yes, I guess you can. Do you have a hand truck? That would make it easier for both of us."

"Sure. Be right back." She took a few steps and then turned. "Don't do it yourself. Wait for me."

Once inside the equipment shed, Carly glanced over her shoulder to make sure he was doing as she said, then grasped the handle of the hand truck, tilted it back on its wheels and rolled it out of the shed, her movements automatic.

She wished Luke had called first so she would have had time to prepare herself, to be the in-charge woman she had worked so hard to become for more than a decade. He didn't have her phone number, but he could have asked Tom or Frances for it. His uncle and aunt knew everyone in the county. In fact, they were hosting the Memorial Day barbecue.

She paused, glancing at Luke. Of course. That's why he was here. He was going to the barbecue, although he'd never attended before. Well, at least she knew. It wouldn't be another surprise. She only wished there wouldn't be so many people there who knew about their past—they'd be watching to see how she and Luke reacted to each other. Her two best friends, Gemma Whitmire and Lisa Thomas, would be at the barbecue, as well. They would help her avoid him if necessary.

"Here we go," she said, all business as she wheeled the hand truck to the back of his pickup. "I want to put the trunk in the house."

Luke jumped into the truck bed and pushed the trunk while Carly pulled. When it was far enough to tilt over the tailgate, he leaped down and helped her lower it to the ground, then onto the hand truck. Together, they rolled it to the house, lifted it up the three shallow steps to the front porch and then through the door into the living room.

Carly moved the coffee table away from the sofa and said, "Here is where I want it."

They moved it into place then stood together, catching their breath.

"I had a couple of guys help me get it into my truck, but we probably should have unpacked it before we moved it." Luke flexed his shoulders. "I don't know what Omi put in there, but it feels like gold bricks."

"Whatever it is, I'll treasure it."

He glanced around the living room, his gaze skimming over the 1940s-style sofa and chair she had reupholstered, the tables and bookcases she had refinished, and the paintings she had unearthed at estate sales and junk shops. She'd painted some of the pictures, too—abstract designs where she'd been playing with color, trying to recreate the feel of a sunset or the exact shade of a field of bluebonnets.

"Yes," he finally said. "I can see that you will. This is very different than what your parents had in here. How are they, by the way?"

"They're doing well now, but slowing down. They took everything with them when my dad got sick and they moved to Tulsa, so I've made the house my own."

"It reminds me of you." The corner of his mouth edged up. "It's cozy. What you always wanted."

And nothing at all like the mansion where he'd been raised in an upscale section of Dallas, and probably nothing like whatever penthouse apartment he now inhabited.

She folded her hands at her waist. "It's the home I wanted to create for myself." Silently she added, *for us*, but those were words she would never speak out loud.

"The place looks great, Carly." Luke started for the door. "You've achieved what your parents tried to do with their organic garden. You've worked hard."

"Thank you." From nowhere a blast of regret and nostalgia swept over her. "I needed to keep busy after we…"

"Yes, of course." Luke opened the door and stepped out. He held it open so she could follow him if she wanted to, but she didn't.

Her only desire was to go huddle in her

chair, to settle into calmness. She couldn't do that, though. She had an order to deliver and a party to attend. She'd been looking forward to that, but now even the thought of the get-together filled her with dread.

"Thank you for delivering the trunk, Luke. I'll take good care of it, and of whatever Wendolin left inside."

"I know you will." He descended the steps then turned back. "Organic gardening? Is that very labor intensive?"

"Of course, but it's worth it because I can honestly say the produce is as fresh, good, and clean as I can make it."

He nodded, as he looked out at her fields again. "I see." He paused again, before he said, "Maybe I'll see you later." With a wave, he strode to his truck, climbed in and drove away.

Grateful the awkward encounter was finished, Carly leaned against the door frame and watched the Oklahoma red dust rise behind his tires then dissipate into the breeze.

Tears sprang into her eyes and she blinked hard to fight them back. Turning, she looked at her legacy from Luke's German-born grandmother, the one who had taught her the importance of cherishing her family, the one who had comforted her when the family she and Luke had tried to create had disappeared in a miscarriage and the cold, silent recriminations that ended their brief marriage.

It all seemed so long ago, and she wouldn't have thought it could still hurt so much. She thought she'd dealt with it, put it behind her, forgiven herself. And him. But maybe facing hurtful memories and being able to forgive were skills that needed to be practiced.

Sitting on the sofa, she ran her fingers over the design of flowers and birds carved into the top of the trunk. This wasn't a piece she would refinish. That would be a travesty. It had come to America with the Bayer family when they fled Nazi Germany eighty years ago, but she didn't know how old it was. The faded paint held only a hint of the beautiful colors that had once decorated the piece and the nicks and scratches spoke of years of everyday use. This had been treasured by Wendolin and her family, and Carly would continue that tradition.

She was tempted to lift the lid to see what

was inside, to examine the precious items that had made it so heavy, but a glance at the clock reminded her she should have left ten minutes ago.

She patted the trunk lid. "I'll be back," she promised.

Hurrying to her bedroom, she grabbed her purse, along with the outfit she would wear to the Sandersons' and a pair of highly polished boots. The restaurant owner to whom she was delivering her produce wouldn't mind if she used their ladies' room to change clothes and freshen up for the party. Gemma and Lisa would probably laugh because she never dressed up, but having seen Luke, she was glad she'd made the decision to do so tonight.

"GLAD THAT'S OVER," Luke murmured as he rolled down the highway toward his aunt and uncle's house. He had done his duty to Omi by delivering the trunk and putting it where Carly wanted it. Now it was time to go see what kinds of jobs Aunt Frances had for him to do before tonight's barbecue.

He couldn't keep his thoughts from returning to Carly, though. The lush prosperity of

Joslin Gardens had been amazing, so different from the scrubby acreage on which her parents had first experimented with organic vegetables. It had been tough going since the ground below the thin topsoil was shale. Luke was sure the garden's current success was entirely due to Carly's hard work.

He'd never forgotten how beautiful she was with her deep brown eyes, strong features and shining black hair, and maturity had made her even more beautiful. He hadn't seen her in all these years—had never been to the annual barbecue—because he hadn't wanted to run into her… He didn't want to bring up bad memories for her, but that's what he'd done this afternoon.

He wouldn't have come this year if he hadn't been caught in circumstances he couldn't change. He would tell her all about it as soon as things were settled. After that, he would deal with the consequences. And the hurt.

THE BARBECUE AT the Sanderson ranch was everything Carly remembered from the past few years, and everything she had hoped it would be this year—crowded, busy and fun. Best of all, the food looked delicious. Frances and her helpers had outdone themselves. Carly took that as a personal favor because she liked to eat and hadn't had anything since breakfast.

The owner of the restaurant where she'd made her delivery had offered to have the cook fix her something, but Carly's only interest had been in changing into her new red skirt and top and pulling on her boots. These were her dancing shoes and she intended to have fun tonight. She deserved it after the jolt she'd received today.

She greeted the people she knew, met a few more, and stood in line at the buffet table. Unashamedly, she filled two plates then turned to look for a place to sit. Spying an empty spot at a table where Lisa Thomas sat with several others, she headed in that direction.

Once she was seated, Lisa turned to her with her eyes wide and spoke quietly. "Did you know Luke is here?" She nodded to a spot across the patio where Luke was talking to his aunt and uncle. The three of them appeared to be deep in a serious discussion.

Tom and Frances Sanderson had held this

barbecue every Memorial Day weekend since they had moved to Reston a few years ago. The news of the property for sale had come from Carly's own father, a longtime acquaintance of Tom's even before his daughter had met and married the Sandersons' nephew. They had proved to be huge assets to the community because they were tireless fundraisers for local causes. Their current passion was reopening the county hospital, which had been closed for several years. Carly knew Tom and Frances had plans to charmingly convince people to donate to the hospital fund, or twist a few arms if necessary.

"Luke?" she asked, bringing her thoughts back to Lisa's question. "Yes. He came to my house."

Lisa's eyes rounded. "Seriously? Why?"

Around bites of food, Carly told her about the trunk.

"Wendolin remembered you in her will? How sweet. She was a wonderful person."

"She was." Carly smiled as she remembered. "So warm and funny…and random."

Lisa smiled. "Yes, I remember the stories you told Gemma and me of how she'd start one thing, abandon it, start another, come back to the first, go to another."

"Somehow she got a great deal done. Usually helping other people. And she was always fun to be around, even if her way of thinking was confusing." Carly sighed. "She was delightful."

Her eyes full of laughter, she asked, "Did I tell you about how she used to go to the end of her sidewalk every day and blow kisses to the kids on the school buses that went by?"

Lisa snickered. "Yes, and one day she failed to notice the passing bus wasn't bright yellow and blew kisses to a load of county prisoners heading to pick up trash on the side of the highway. That must have been the best part of their day."

"No doubt. She was a little…odd, but in the sweetest way. I'm sure she was the best thing in Luke's life for the past dozen years."

"Oh, why do you say that?"

Carly chewed thoughtfully, "Because after his mother died, she was the biggest positive female influence in his life—"

"Until he met you."

Carly gave a small shrug. "We both know

that didn't turn out to be very positive for him."

"Not your fault," Lisa insisted.

Carly knew that wasn't true, but she didn't want to talk about it anymore. She was grateful when Lisa's attention was snagged by someone else.

Before Carly had finished eating, Lisa and a couple of people left the table and others took their places. Carly looked up from her salad to see Luke, along with Tom and Frances, settling into chairs opposite her. Both men were looking anxiously at Frances, whose face had gone pale.

CHAPTER TWO

"WHAT WERE YOU THINKING, Frannie?" Tom fussed at his wife as he handed her a glass of ice water. "When was the last time you had something to drink or eat?"

"Right now," she answered, dutifully gulping some water and then digging into the food Luke placed in front of her.

Once Tom and Luke were sure she was eating, they glanced around the table. Luke gave a start when his gaze met Carly's.

"Oh, hi." He inclined his head. "Didn't see you here."

"I wouldn't miss this," Carly answered. Since she'd had a minute to steel herself, she was able to give them a genuine smile. "It's the real start of summer and the food—" she moved her fork in a circular motion "—is incredible."

Frances looked from Carly to Luke then smiled. "Thank you, dear. I have to say what we've prepared has only been enhanced by your fresh produce. Your suggestion of grilled zucchini spiced with red pepper was inspired. Everyone seems to love it."

"I know my people. Around here, spicy always sells. Having alternative zucchini recipes helps me sell the overabundance, which has only increased with all the rain we've been having. And then there's the fact that my squash plants don't know a thing about birth control."

Frances and Tom laughed and Luke's eyes crinkled at the corners when he grinned at her.

This isn't too bad, Carly thought. She could do this, no problem. She could sit and chat with this lovely couple and her own ex-husband, make small talk while stuffing her face. She took a bite of the cauliflower salad, savoring the tang of the Parmesan cheese.

There were two other people at the table, Roland and Becky Hall, whom she had known all her life. They were certainly aware of her long-ago marriage to Luke, but they wouldn't bring it up.

Becky looked at Frances and said, "Thank

you so much for inviting us. We haven't been able to come in previous years, but we're so glad we could make it this time. I love getting to know people. Where are you and your husband from originally, and how did you meet?"

"She's a born romantic," Roland contributed. "She loves this kind of stuff."

"We're from a small town about fifty miles from Houston," Tom answered. "So we're transplanted Texans."

"We always knew each other growing up," Frances added. "Although Tom is far, far older than I am."

"Two years!" he objected, drawing a laugh from everyone.

Frances put down her fork and reached over to take her husband's hand. "He'd been asking me out for a year…"

"And she always turned me down. I think I scared her." Tom shook his head as if he was still mystified by that.

"You definitely scared me. You were so serious. Until prom. I thought that would be a safe date, not too awkward, lots of other people around. I could hide out in the girls' restroom with my friends if need be… And then the staircase happened."

"The staircase?" Luke, who obviously hadn't heard this story before, looked from his aunt to his uncle.

"The prom was held at a beautiful ballroom a couple of towns over from ours. It had a big, sweeping staircase and all of us had to give our tickets to someone at the top of the stairs, have our picture taken together, or with our friends, and then go down to the ballroom."

Frances paused for effect and sipped her water, her eyes laughing over the rim.

"And?" Carly prompted when she couldn't stand the suspense. "What happened?"

"I was wearing my first pair of real high heels."

Carly and Becky groaned.

"For days, I had practiced walking and dancing in those four-inch nightmares. I paid my little brother to be my dance partner. But it never occurred to me to practice going up and down stairs. After we got our picture taken, we turned to start down the steps." Frances winced. "My heel caught on the carpet, my foot came right out of the shoe and

I pitched forward." Frances made tumbling motions with her hands. "I somersaulted all the way to the bottom without stopping—"

"While I rushed along trying to catch her, but she was moving too fast."

The breathless audience stared as Luke asked, "Aunt Frances, were you hurt?"

"Only my pride," she answered on a sigh. "I lay there staring at the ceiling, trying to get my breath back, and this man—" she gave Tom a loving look "—this man whipped a twenty-dollar bill out of his wallet and said, 'You win the bet, Frances. I didn't think you'd have the nerve to prove you're head over heels for me.'"

Everyone broke into laughter and applause.

"I was the belle of the ball," she concluded. "And I was so sore the next few days I could hardly move. I learned my lesson, though. I haven't worn four-inch heels since."

"Best twenty bucks I ever spent," Tom said smugly. "We got married six years later." He leaned over and kissed his wife, who happily kissed him back.

"I'm only glad I wasn't the cause of you taking that tumble," he went on. "I was so awkward and nervous, I'm surprised it wasn't *my* feet you tripped over. You never would have gone out with me again."

"Absolutely true," Frances said.

Carly's gaze flew to Luke. He was looking at his relatives with pride and humor, but he must have felt her attention on him because he turned his eyes to meet hers. A shadow passed over his features and he twisted away.

She and Luke certainly didn't have a story like that, full of drama, but also sweetness. Theirs had consisted of overwhelming attraction, pain and recriminations.

Suddenly desperate to get away, Carly began gathering her silverware and stacking it on top of her two empty plates. "If you'll excuse me, everyone, I know Frances's chocolate cake is over on the dessert table and it's eager to be my new best friend. I think I'll take a piece into a dark corner and show it some appreciation."

Becky smiled as she asked, "Cake, too? Sounds wonderful. I wish I could eat like that."

"You might have to work as hard as Carly

does," Luke said. "She owns Joslin Gardens and does most of the work herself."

"Oh, that's right," Becky said, giving a small wave of her hand as if to shoo away her previous error. "I knew that. And you refinish furniture, too, right? I've been looking for a small table and a couple of chairs for my breakfast nook. The one I've got is too big and too modern-looking for my house. I like retro."

Even though she wanted to get away, Carly couldn't resist an opportunity to talk about her other business. "As a matter of fact, I do. I recently completed a rebuild of a little gate-leg table with two chairs. I painted it pale yellow. It looks like something straight out of the 1950s."

"Sounds perfect," Becky said. "When can I see it?"

They arranged a time for her to come out to Joslin Gardens and Carly was at last able to stand and begin making her escape, but she stopped when Tom asked, "You're going to open a shop in town, right? To sell your furniture and other pieces?"

"That's right, although I haven't settled on

a space yet. I'm calling it Upcycle because everything will be reclaimed and repurposed."

"Excellent," Becky said. "I'll probably be a regular customer." Her husband squawked an objection and she gave him a playful punch on the arm. She turned her smile on Luke. "And what about you? Will you be going back to Dallas after the holiday?"

He sat back, stretched out his legs and looked at Carly as he said, "I'll be around for a few days, then back to Dallas. I am buying property in this area, though."

Carly's face felt as frozen as a Siberian lake in winter. Her heart pounded and a wave of distress swept over her. She hoped that didn't mean he planned to buy a house nearby. If he did, she might run into him anytime.

DISMAYED, LUKE WATCHED as Carly gave everyone at the table a bright smile. "It's always nice to have more people in Reston," she said before she hurried away. The Halls followed a few minutes later, heading toward the dessert table, as well.

He hadn't meant to spring it on her like that. He'd only decided today, when he'd received the reports from the engineers, that Reston would be the perfect place for his project.

"Well, that wasn't as awkward as it could have been," Frances said, her sympathetic gaze following Carly.

"It was awkward enough, and I suppose I could have told her before I made a general announcement."

"I wouldn't worry about it," his uncle said. "Carly's so busy, you'll probably never see her." Tom paused. "I'm glad you're going to be here for a while. How long will your project take?"

"Dad's given me nine months—"

"Because he thinks you can't do it in that length of time, and then you'll come back to Dallas with your tail between your legs." Tom shook his head. "My brother still thinks a vacancy is going to occur and he'll be king of the world."

Luke nodded and gave an ironic twist of his lips. "True, but that's another reason I'm glad I can buy the property I need from you." He paused. "The location, though…" He ran his hand over his chin.

"It has everything you need, Luke. The right layers of shale, privacy—"

"A crummy road to keep people out," Frances added.

"Although it will have to be graded so we can get the equipment in and out," Luke answered.

"And you won't have a fight over the mineral rights." Tom grimaced. "Or the ones on the adjoining property."

"*That's* what I'm worried about."

"I know, but you don't have time to look for another place, not with my brother breathing down your neck." Tom held out his scarred rancher's hands, palms up. "I don't see what else you can do."

"Me neither," Luke answered in a dull voice.

All three brooded over the situation for a moment before Frances stood and said, "I think it's time for me to start making the rounds and charming people out of their money." She smiled when she spied her daughter-in-law carrying her baby son across the patio. "Good. Max is up from his nap. I'll take our grandson along as my sidekick."

As she swept away in a swirl of brightly colored skirt, Tom watched her go and said, "Marrying her was the smartest thing I ever did."

Glad for the change of subject, Luke nodded. "I agree." He fell silent, mulling over the fact that so many of his family members had happy marriages, successful relationships. His parents had been happy, even though they were completely different people—his mother had been sweet and easy-going, his dad was…well, tough. All indications were that his Omi, Wendolin, had been happy with her husband, Harry, who had died when Luke was twelve. The rest of the family seemed happy, too. Not only Tom and Frances, but their son, Trent, and his wife, Mia, their lives even more complete now that they had Max.

He fought a surge of envy, knowing that he and Carly and their disastrous marriage, as well as the loss of their baby, were the exception that proved the rule in his family.

He also knew that he was slipping very close to feeling sorry for himself. Standing, he went to snag a piece of Aunt Frances's cake before it was all gone.

THIS WAS THE perfect time. He wiggled under the barbed-wire fence and reached back for the bucket whose handle he'd wrapped with cloth so it wouldn't make noise if it fell. Now he just had to make sure he didn't drop the bucket itself, especially not after he filled it with what he needed.

Bent at the waist and keeping his head low, he scuttled down the rows of spring onions, carrots and beets. He wasn't interested in those. He stopped at the blueberry bushes and carefully opened the wood-and-chicken-wire lid of the first protective cage built to keep the animals from eating the berries.

No one had expected a two-legged animal to show up and help himself, he thought, and grinned in the light of the full moon. He wasn't being greedy, he assured himself. They had plenty and he planned to take only a few from each bush. That way, there would be enough left for tomorrow night. Working quickly, he filled his bucket, closed the cages and disappeared into the night.

CHAPTER THREE

THE NEXT MORNING, Carly stood on the lane that sloped north to south across her fields and watched her employees as they picked and loaded produce. Everyone seemed to be moving in slow motion this morning. Probably due to the Memorial Day holiday. Any kind of break in the routine seemed to throw her teenage helpers off their stride. The delivery to the Mustang Supermarket would be late today, but she'd called to tell the manager about the delay. Now she needed to not stress over it.

She couldn't blame the holiday weekend for her sleepless night or the edginess that had awakened her with the first light of dawn and sent her roaming the fields for peace. She couldn't stop thinking about Luke and the fact that he was going to be around Reston. She didn't know how long he would be staying—although his mention of buying property certainly suggested a lengthy stay—or when she would see him again, but she dreaded it.

Turning back toward her equipment shed, she took a deep breath and worked to quell the anxious flutter that had started in her stomach. She didn't want to think about Luke, and she hated being late or appearing unreliable. That was why she had resisted Lisa and Gemma's efforts to get her to open a shop in which to sell her recycled goods. Keeping up the stock, finding old pieces to transform into new ones, having regular shop hours had all seemed overwhelming until her friends had convinced her to at least give it a try. If it was too much or if the shop was unsuccessful, they'd argued, she could go back to posting her pieces online and either shipping them or having the new owners pick them up.

She didn't like the idea of quitting if her shop didn't succeed. Giving up wasn't in her nature. She had only ever given up on one thing in her life—marriage to Luke—and that wasn't a decision she'd made alone.

For the new shop, Lisa had helped her find a couple of reliable employees and Carly had hired more help for her gardens to free her up for the shop. She only hoped her newest commercial enterprise didn't turn out to be a huge mistake.

For some reason she'd been feeling restless lately, ready to take on something new but not sure what that would be. Her two best friends thought she was a little crazy to work so hard when she was finally in a position to hire more employees, but she'd developed the habit when she'd returned to Reston after she and Luke had broken up. She had recovered from her double heartbreak by spending days in the fields or the greenhouse and evenings refinishing furniture. All that labor had consumed her time and thoughts, and exhausted her so much that she'd fallen into dreamless sleep every night. Now those habits were so ingrained she couldn't change.

She walked up to the front of the shed as Jay and Sheena arrived, driving four-wheeled utility vehicles pulling garden carts full of vegetables. They began loading the produce into the big plastic bins she used for deliveries and stacking them carefully in the back of her truck while Carly hurried inside to brush her hair into a ponytail, slather on sunscreen and plop a wide-brimmed hat onto her head.

As she passed through the living room, she gave Wendolin's trunk a yearning glance. She was eager to open it and begin going through the contents. It would bring her closer to the sweet woman she had known, and it might help her put parts of her long-ago marriage to Luke into perspective. Even after all this time, she still didn't fully understand some of the things that had happened. Tonight, she promised herself. She would open it tonight.

By the time she returned to the shed, the kids had the produce loaded and Jay was ready to go. Watching them work as she hurried from the house, Carly thought again how lucky she was to have these two working for her. There were two other occasional employees who operated her produce stand, but they didn't have the work ethic of Sheena and Jay.

Sheena Blake was the oldest of five children of a single mom and needed to earn money to help out at home. She was pretty in a quiet and earnest way, and willing to work.

Jay Morton was the son of the mayor of Reston, and he'd been raised to be a hard worker. She knew he liked video games and electronic devices. A couple of times she had caught him playing games on his phone when he should have been sorting and packing produce but, for the most part, he was a good employee.

Carly smiled as she handed Sheena the clipboard with the paperwork Jay would need. He was eager to get going, finish this job and go on to the next one, while Sheena was fixated on double-checking everything. Carly feared that her own meticulous habits were beginning to affect the girl.

"Don't drive too fast," she said to Jay. "I don't know where all the extra people have come from, but traffic in town seems heavier than usual."

"I know, Carly. I just came from town," he said, nodding toward the motorcycle he rode everywhere. He shook his head and exchanged looks with Sheena as if he thought their persnickety boss was losing her mind. Sheena smiled back as color rushed into her face.

"Oh, of course." Carly gave him the keys. As he pulled out, she and Sheena went back to work, picking the remainder of the vegetables they needed to deliver today and getting them ready to go. Carly was grateful for the manual labor that left her too busy to think about yesterday's encounters with Luke.

When they took a break, Sheena took a long drink of water from one of the bottles Carly always kept in a cooler in the shed, then poured some into her hand and splashed it on her face. Once she was cooled off, she turned troubled eyes to Carly. "Have you seen Mrs. Salyer lately?"

Carly paused, trying to remember the last time she'd seen her elderly neighbor. "No, not in a few weeks. Why?"

"My mom stopped to see her yesterday and she said Mrs. Salyer was in bed. In the middle of the day."

"Era wasn't sewing or gardening or…putting a new roof on her house?"

"No. Mom said it looks like Mrs. Salyer didn't even put in a garden this year."

"Is she sick?"

"She said she's just tired. At least, that's what she told Mom."

"I'd better check on her." Hearing that Era Salyer was napping instead of working was like learning the sun had decided not to rise one morning. It simply didn't happen. "Can you finish up here?"

"Sure."

Carly scooped her cell phone out of her pocket and called Era, but there was no answer. She grabbed a basket and filled it with fresh produce.

Carly hurried to one of the four-wheelers and rode down the highway, being careful to keep her slower vehicle at the edge of the pavement.

At the mailbox marked Salyer, she turned in and made her way over the rutted lane, which wasn't in much better shape than her own. She stopped in front of Era's small house, noting the unaccustomed sight of dry and drooping roses and hydrangeas. At the side of the house, the plot that usually held Era's lush vegetable garden was choked with weeds.

Carly hurried to the front door. A scuffling noise followed her knock and, after a pause, Era called out, "Who is it?"

"It's Carly Joslin, Mrs. Salyer. I haven't seen you in a while so I wanted to see how you're doing."

Instead of opening the door wide as was her custom and embracing her, Era opened it only as far as the guard chain would allow and peeped out.

"Oh, hi, Carly. How are you?"

"I'm fine. It's you I'm worried about." Carly tried to look past the older lady, but could see nothing in the dim room—a room whose windows had always been open to light and air. She brought her attention back to Era, noting that her face seemed thinner.

"I'm fine. Nothing wrong with me, honey. Just a little tired."

Carly held up the basket. "I brought you some vegetables and some berries."

Era frowned. "Berries? Oh, I thought you already left me some…"

When her voice trailed off, Carly asked, "Thought I left you what?"

"Oh, oh, nothing. I…don't know what I was going to say." She looked up and smiled. "Thank you, honey. Just leave it on the porch. I don't want to open the door because… I might have a cold and I don't want to get you sick, too."

Carly blinked and did as the older lady asked, setting down the basket as she said, "Era, please let me know if you need anything. Really, anything at all."

"I will, hon. Thank you."

Before Carly could say another thing, Era closed the door. The dead bolt clicked into place.

Puzzled, Carly walked slowly to her four-wheeler.

"This is so strange," she whispered. She couldn't recall a single time when Era had behaved this way. A widow for many years, she had lost her only son to an oilfield accident a few years ago. In spite of those hardships, she had always seemed content with her life. She was hardworking and independent and had been friendly and welcoming to her neighbors.

Carly couldn't think of anything that would have caused such a change in her, unless she really was sick.

She glanced over her shoulder to see that Era was holding back one of the living room curtains to give a reassuring wave and a smile.

It was as if she didn't want Carly around but didn't want her to worry, either.

Deciding to call again in a few days, or to send someone, Carly drove home and reported the visit to Sheena, who said she would tell her mom about it.

Jay returned from town with the truck and the three of them were finished by noon. Since Sheena lived on the outskirts of Reston, less than three miles away, she rode home on her bicycle, leaving Carly and Jay to load the last delivery onto the truck.

When they were done, she said, "Jay, I can take this to the restaurant. I've got to go into Toncaville, anyway."

He grinned. "Did your favorite second-hand store get a new delivery of beat-up furniture?"

Teasingly, she narrowed her eyes at him. "I think you've been working for me too long. You know me too well."

"Yeah, I've been meaning to talk to you about that. I'm pretty sure I deserve a raise."

She only laughed and waved him off as he

mounted his motorcycle, but he paused before putting on his helmet. "Um, Carly, did you pick any of the blueberries yet?"

"Only a few to take to Mrs. Salyer. She loves my berries. Why?"

"I don't know, just seems like there aren't as many on the bushes as there were a few days ago." He rubbed his chin, where he was attempting to grow his scraggly few whiskers into a beard. "'Course, it might be rabbits, skunks, squirrels."

"Animals that can open the protective chicken-wire cages?" Carly asked.

"Nah, I guess not. Besides, I didn't see any tracks." With a shrug, Jay put on his helmet, started the engine and roared away.

Carly smiled as she watched him go. A raise was in the near future, but she wasn't quite sure when it would happen. He was a good employee and she was going to miss him when he went to college in the fall of next year. In the meantime, she would take a look at the blueberry bushes, as soon as she got the chance.

After making sure the produce was shielded from the sun beneath a damp cloth,

Carly rushed inside to shower and change for the trip into town.

When she opened her closet, she didn't grab shorts to go with the turquoise tank top she'd pulled over her head, but instead took out a dark purple peasant skirt with an asymmetrical hem that fell to midcalf.

She held it up and admired the beautiful color. Lisa had dragged her to Tulsa on a shopping spree, insisting that Carly needed to wear something besides work clothes and boots. Carly had argued she had nowhere to wear skirts like this. Lisa, who worked in real estate and dressed up every day, insisted she could invent a reason.

"Invent a reason?" Carly had asked.

Looking at the beautiful skirt now, Carly thought there was no reason to wear it. She would only be dropping vegetables off at a restaurant, then making a quick stop at The Classy Junque Trunk to look for items she could freshen up and resell at Upcycle—once she actually decided on a space.

She slipped it on and twirled in front of the mirror. No reason to wear such a dressy skirt, except that she loved it and sometimes, like last night, she needed to dress like a girl. Grabbing her purse, she hurried outside, locked the door and turned around, only to see Luke Sanderson's truck stopped beside hers and him stepping out.

CHAPTER FOUR

LUKE REMOVED HIS sunglasses and his gaze swept over her as he smiled. "Hi, Carly. Hope you don't mind that I stopped by again."

Her surprise at seeing him gave way to an unexpected flush of heat. "Um, well, no," she said, but she frowned uncertainly. There was no way to stop him. There wasn't a gate on her drive, no fence across the front where she could attach one.

"Good." As he stepped forward he removed an envelope from his shirt pocket and handed it to her. "There's something I need to talk to you about, and I forgot to give you this when I brought the trunk. It's from my grandmother and it's addressed to both of us." He gave a small shrug and the corner of his mouth kicked up. "We're supposed to open it together, but it looks like you're getting ready to go somewhere."

"I have a delivery in Toncaville, then I have a stop to make before I come back here."

"Maybe we could set a time and I could come back tomorrow." He watched her, his light brown eyes steady.

"Um, yes, that might be best or..." She glanced down at her dressy skirt. Maybe seeing him again was short-circuiting her common sense, or maybe this was her day for snap decisions. Anxiety tightened her chest but she took a deep breath to calm herself and considered what to do. She didn't want to see him again, didn't want the possibility of him returning tomorrow hanging over her head. She knew he was going to come back to this area but didn't want to see him then, either. On the other hand, she owed a huge debt to Wendolin. Carly tried to manufacture a smile. "Or you could come along with me. You could read the letter and we could talk about it."

"Sounds like a plan." He pressed the button on his key fob to lock his truck and walked over to open the driver's door on hers, standing back while she slid behind the wheel, then striding around to climb in beside her.

Carly started the truck, taking a moment to be grateful that Jay had cleaned it out earlier, making sure there was no mud on the seat and sweeping up most of the dried bits of grass and plant matter on the floor.

As they pulled onto the road and headed in the direction of Toncaville, Luke turned toward her and lifted his knee onto the seat. Settling back, he slipped a finger beneath the flap of the envelope and opened it carefully. He pulled out the letter, but before he unfolded it, he saw that there was bold writing on the outside of the last page.

"'Dear Bonbon,'" he started, but was interrupted by a snicker from Carly.

"I never knew Wendolin called you Bonbon," she said, sending him an amused glance.

Luke's eyebrows drew together in a pained expression. "I begged her not to and she stopped for a long time, but she probably figured that since this was the last thing she would write to me, she could call me whatever she wanted."

"No doubt." She nodded toward the paper. "Go ahead."

Luke returned to the letter. "'Dear Bon-bon, be sure you and Carly unpack the trunk together.'"

Carly took her eyes off the road for a second to stare at him. "That's it?"

"That's it."

How much more complicated was this going to get? she wondered, but she said, "We should honor her last wishes. We can take care of it this evening." She glanced at the dashboard clock, wondering if there was time to turn around and take Luke back to his truck. There wasn't. "I have to make this delivery in Toncaville and I don't want to be late because this is a new customer, so you'll still have to come with me."

"That fits right in with my plans," he said, facing forward and stretching out his legs. "My uncle was making noises this morning about me helping him build an outdoor play set for Max. The kid's not even a year old, can't walk yet. How's he going to climb the thing?"

"Knowing your knack for free styling on building projects, Tom was probably counting on you to come up with something."

Luke grinned. "Like a baby elevator to take him to the top of the slide." He thought about it for a second. "A little chair attached to a pulley would work. Have to have a safety harness and a crank that can be operated easily."

"Now you're talking." Carly took a breath. This wasn't so hard, and having him along, talking so easily like this, helped her quell her anxiety about the lateness of today's deliveries. She spent so much time alone, working in her gardens or various refurbishing projects, it felt good to have someone else along—or at least that was what she was telling herself.

Luke gave her a sidelong glance. "So you remember how I like to improvise on building projects, huh?"

"Yes, I do." She also recalled that when they were first married, they had talked about buying a house—a fixer-upper they could remodel the way they wanted it—or even building one themselves. A home where they could raise their child. Instead they had lived in a high-rise in Dallas, a sharp-angles-and-glass creation owned by his father's corporation. It had been completely unsuited to Carly's interests and nature, but she'd thought they wouldn't be there very long. In fact, it was the only place they'd ever lived together.

Luke was looking out his window, watching the pine trees zip past. He was relaxed, at ease, his hand wrapped around the flip-down handle above the door, fingers drumming on the hard plastic. She needed to try to be the same.

She knew it was silly—a woman of thirty-two, who made a point of seeming happy and carefree, becoming twisted with anxiety about a late delivery. She had worked so long on her own, though, been responsible for every detail of her business, that she found it almost impossible to relax about any part of it. She knew she needed to be calmer, to take things easier.

She spotted a small, dark figure ahead and slammed on the brakes.

"Whoa." Luke shot his hand out to steady himself against the dashboard. "What is it, Carly?"

She put the truck in Park, hit the hazard lights and vaulted from the cab—or would have if she hadn't become tangled in her full skirt. With a sound of annoyance, she tugged it out of the way and jumped out.

"I'll be right back," she called over her shoulder as she slammed the door.

LUKE STEPPED OUT as Carly darted up the road. Several yards in front of the truck, she stooped to pick something up. When she turned, he saw it was a turtle. Holding it with a hand on each side of the shell, she hurried across the road and carefully set the reptile down in the bar ditch. She watched it for a minute, then nodded. She turned back to the truck but stopped suddenly when she saw that he was only a few feet behind her.

He pointed to the turtle, which was slowly climbing out of the ditch to make his way across the field.

"What was that all about?"

"Saving a life," she answered breezily. "Come on."

He paused and stared after her, but when it looked like she wasn't going to offer any further explanation—or wait for him—he hurried after her, swinging into the truck as she started to roll.

Luke fastened his seat belt and was on the verge of asking about the turtle when she stopped again. This time, though, there were two turtles. When she said, "Help me," he followed, snatching up one of the creatures at the moment a car zipped past, causing him to stumble back. Recovering his balance and giving the driver an annoyed look, he followed her to the bar ditch, but this time to the opposite side from where she'd carried the last one.

The turtle craned its head from one side to another as it opened and closed its mouth. Looking at Carly, Luke asked, "Are you on a one-woman turtle rescue crusade?"

"Yes, but they're actually tortoises. The one you're carrying is called a snapping turtle, but it's a tortoise."

He set it down hastily. "Can't they get across the road by themselves? They seemed to be doing okay."

"Did you see how fast that car was going?" she asked with an indignant wave of her hand. "These tortoises can't move fast enough to get across the road before being hit by a maniac like that. Every year at this time it's the same thing—tortoises are moving around, crossing the road, and many of them get run over. It makes me sick. I think some people deliberately aim for them." She paused and stood, watching the two animals.

"What are you waiting for?"

"Making sure they're heading away from the road, not back onto it."

She stood with her hands on her hips, bending slightly to watch the rescues inch out of the ditch and into the field beside it. He suspected that if Carly had more time, and had been wearing something other than a skirt and dressy sandals, she would have climbed through the split-rail cedar fence and carried them much farther away from the asphalt.

That was one thing that hadn't changed. Carly wanted to see things set right. Her friend Gemma had been the one who had rescued animals, but Carly had helped find them homes and then gone back to check to make sure the animals were well cared for.

He remembered how she would become enraged over some injustice she'd seen on the local news and talk about ways to solve the issue. He also never forgot how she'd turned heads when they were out together. Her striking looks drew other men's attention like magnets swinging toward true north. He'd felt extremely proud and intensely jealous. His comeuppance had come with a vengeance when they'd split up and he'd been stopped cold any time he'd seen a tall, black-haired woman with a loose-hipped walk striding down the street. He'd almost followed a couple of them, thinking it was Carly, knowing he wouldn't so much as say hello. Of course, it never had been her. Gemma and Lisa had swept her back home to Reston so she could recover and escape the misery he'd caused. Eventually he'd had to leave Dallas because the memories were so hard and his pining for her so sharp.

Looking at her now, gazing intently at two tortoises who didn't know how to keep themselves safe, he experienced echoes of that hunger. When they'd met, she had been as clueless about self-protection as those tortoises. At twenty-one, he'd been cocky, chasing adventures and experiences, determined to get what he'd wanted, and as soon as he'd seen Carly, she was what he wanted.

It hadn't been until years later, working

on a construction project in Venezuela, that he'd finally acknowledged that his frenetic thirst for escapades had been nothing more than an attempt to outrun his grief over the unexpected death of his mother when he was eighteen. He'd done the same thing after the miscarriage of their child and the end of their short marriage.

The realization had come between one hammer blow on a nail head and the next. He'd collapsed onto the ground so suddenly and completely, a fellow carpenter had come running, thinking he'd been injured.

But instead he'd taken the first step toward dealing with his grief for his mom, his child, and for the way he'd screwed up with Carly.

Now he was back. They had both moved on with their lives, but he felt he owed her something. An apology? The ones he'd offered years ago had never really plumbed the depths of his regret. Reparations, which he knew she'd never accept? A child? Impossible. He couldn't turn back time.

Finally satisfied with the reptiles' progress, Carly waved him toward the truck, snapping him out of his solemn reverie.

"Let's go," she commanded. "I've got a delivery to make."

Luke grinned as he shook his head. "Then maybe you'd better put the tortoise rescues on hold. We're still about twenty minutes from Toncaville, aren't we?"

She answered with a stern look that made him laugh even more as she started the truck and pulled onto the highway once again. "Well, maybe we won't see any more."

"Maybe."

They stopped three more times, but Luke jumped out while she was still rolling and moved the endangered tortoise out of the way. By the time they reached the Toncaville city limits, they had their routine down to about two minutes per stop.

"So, I'm guessing we'll be doing the same thing on the way back home," he said, watching her face.

"Absolutely." She smiled at him. "Thanks, Luke. I've hardly ever had help with this before, except when Lisa or Gemma is riding with me. Mostly, my garden helpers will assist in the rescues, but if they're afraid of being seen by their friends, they'll laugh at me and wait while I finish running back and forth across the highway."

"You're welcome. Say, I haven't had lunch yet. How about you?"

"No. I was going to grab something here in town."

"Why don't you let me buy you lunch?" he asked as she pulled into the parking lot at the back of the restaurant where she was delivering her produce. "This looks like a good place."

"It is." She hesitated as she stepped out and walked to the back of the truck, where he joined her.

He knew it wasn't a good idea and he was sure she knew it, too. Riding in the truck, talking about the passing scenery, hustling tortoises out of danger, was one thing. Sitting in a restaurant, eating a meal, seemed too…intimate, even though they had certainly shared meals before, including last night's barbecue. Besides, although it was three o'clock in the afternoon and there wouldn't be many customers in the place, it might seem like they were a couple—then he wondered if she actually cared about that. She seemed so completely sure of herself now. Maybe she wasn't affected by gossip.

She smiled at him. "The chef, Beth Orwin, makes the best grilled trout in southeastern Oklahoma."

"And we already know that she buys the best produce around." He pulled back the cool, damp cloth and picked up a bin full of lettuce and other vegetables. He looked down at the fat, red radishes, bright orange carrots and cream-colored parsnips. "These are beautiful, you know."

To his surprise, her cheeks flushed and she hitched up one shoulder in a slight shrug. "I always think of them as jewels uncovered in the earth. Silly, I know."

"Not at all."

"I guess we *should* try some of my vegetables," she admitted. "I mean, quality control and all that."

"Yes, we should."

They unloaded the truck, took care of the paperwork and then walked around to the front entrance.

Luke marveled at how things had changed in twenty-four hours. Yesterday at about this time, he had been nervously pulling onto her property, worrying that she wouldn't talk to him. He wouldn't have blamed her if that had been the case, but he had known she would accept what Wendolin had left her. He only had to remember to keep this light and casual. They would eat lunch, run any errands she needed to take care of, then go back to unpack the trunk. He wasn't sure why his grandmother had wanted him to be involved with this, but he was determined to follow her instructions. He owed it to her, but he also owed it to Carly to stay away from her. He already knew how much he could hurt her.

Luke gave her a regretful glance. His heart sank because he knew he was about to do it again.

THIS WASN'T AS easy as she'd thought it would be. In fact, it was much harder. They had eaten a late lunch then talked to Beth, the chef and owner of the restaurant, who praised the vegetables and ordered more. Carly had decided to forget the stop at her favorite junk store. Her usual routine of digging through their ratty stock wasn't something she wanted to do while Luke tagged along. Besides, she wasn't dressed for it, which she hadn't really considered when she'd put on this fancy skirt. So, after they ate, they had returned to Joslin Gardens, the drive interrupted by three more stops to rescue tortoises.

Carly was able to control her edginess by focusing on returning home. She and Luke took the empty vegetable bins into the shed where Sheena would rinse them before they were used again. Once they were inside the house, they washed their hands then went to the living room, where the trunk awaited them. Luke slipped the letter out of his pocket and laid it on an end table within easy reach.

The lid wasn't hinged, but separated completely from the body of the trunk. Luke set it aside, then came to sit by Carly on the sofa. The first item they removed was wrapped in yellowed tissue paper that Carly peeled back carefully to reveal satin and lace, also yellowed with age.

Luke ran a hand over the smooth fabric. "Is this...?"

"Wendolin's wedding dress, I'll bet," Carly

said, lifting it out reverently to unfold it. "She gave us her wedding dress."

"I had no idea she still had it. I've never seen it before. I'm her only grandchild, so I guess it makes sense it would come to me." Luke's eyes twinkled. "I don't think it will fit me, though."

Carly rolled her eyes at him, refolded the dress and set it aside. Beneath it were textiles, finely woven tablecloths and napkins, some embroidered in bright colors, one set with exquisitely detailed cutwork embroidery.

"These are beautiful. Perfect, in fact," Carly said. "Family heirlooms."

"And they're all yours, Carly. I would never use them." He glanced around her living room then gestured toward the embroidered cloth covering an old table that had been one of her thrift-store discoveries. "And it's obvious you would."

"Thank you. I'll treasure them."

Carly found many other packets of letters and she was wildly curious to know what they said, but she couldn't read German and they weren't from her family, so she knew they weren't her business. Instead, she reached for a cardboard tube about fourteen inches long. It was very heavy and had a cloth stuffed tightly into each end.

"I wonder what this is."

"One way to find out," Luke said, tugging the fabric at one end and pushing it at the other. "Here, hold on to the tube."

As instructed, she gripped the tube with both hands while he worked to free the wrapped object. By wiggling and twisting it, he managed to pull it out. He handed it to Carly, who placed it on the sofa between them and began unwrapping the layers.

"This is silk," she said at one point, rubbing the red, white and black cloth between her fingers.

"This is a flag," Luke added, pointing out the grommets where it would be attached to a flagpole.

When Carly pulled away the last fold of silk, they discovered there was yet another layer of cotton batting, which they also lifted off.

"Oh, my goodness," Carly breathed, staring at the bronze statue they had revealed. "It's a little girl. Isn't she beautiful?"

The figure was twelve inches high and depicted a child of about seven years old. One hand was held up in front of her face and a butterfly rested lightly on her palm. The wonder and delight on the little girl's face was a joy to see.

Carly examined the base and bottom to locate the artist's name but couldn't read the faint markings. "Whoever did this was a master craftsman. The attention to detail is amazing. You can even see her eyelashes and the lunules on her fingernails. See?" She pointed out the half-moon shapes at the base of each nail. "And the hands are perfectly done, the mark of a talented artist." She ran the tip of her calloused finger over the delicate hands. "Is it Wendolin as a little girl?"

Luke shrugged. "I think so, but I'm not sure. I have a few pictures of Omi when she was little, but they're not very clear. Whoever the family photographer was, he felt obligated to stand at the top of the most distant hill to get everyone in the picture, so there are no close-ups of anyone's face." He held up the fabric that had been wrapped around the statue. "This is definitely a flag, pre–World War II German. I wonder why this was used."

"Maybe they kept the flag because they were giving up their country but not their nationality. Seriously, Wendolin never talked to you about this?"

"Very little. I remember her saying she wasn't brave, but I never knew what she meant by that."

They both looked at the statue again and Carly ran her hand over the flag. "It's possible, too, that if the statue is valuable, someone wanted to make sure it was wrapped in natural fabrics rather than synthetics…" She paused. "Although, now that I think about it, the 1930s weren't exactly rife with nylon and, of course, polyester wasn't created until 1941."

Luke grinned and raised his eyebrows at her. "I wouldn't know and I have to wonder how you do."

She shrugged. "I must have read it somewhere and it stuck in my head."

Carly ran her fingers over the figure, imagining they were touching soft hair, the fabric of a skirt, the gloss of shiny dress shoes. Although the little girl looked happy, enthralled by the tiny scrap of nature that had lit upon her fingers, the tableau made Carly sad. She glanced up and said as much to Luke.

"Why sad?" Luke asked.

"I'm not sure, except that it's a moment frozen in time and…and Wendolin moved on from this beautiful moment and never recaptured it. Maybe it's not so much sadness I'm feeling as it is melancholy or nostalgia."

Luke frowned as he gave the statue a considering look. "Wait a minute, I do remember this. When I was small, it sat on a table in Omi's living room. I wanted to play with it, but, of course, she didn't want me to break it, so she must have put it away then never got it out again, at least, not where I could see it."

Carly cradled it in her hands then looked up with tears spilling from her eyes. "I can't accept this, Luke. It's a family heirloom."

"She wanted you to have it."

Carly went to find a tissue and took several minutes to compose herself. When she returned to the living room, Luke had replaced everything in the trunk and put the lid on.

The statue stood in the middle, a happy little girl, frozen in time.

"Thanks, Luke," she said through trembling lips. "I'll always treasure it."

"I know."

Luke reached into his pocket and took out his keys.

Carly felt an unexpected surge of relief. Although she'd been anxious since Luke's arrival, she had tamped down the strongest feelings of regret, sorrow and angry betrayal. She had thought those feelings had been conquered long ago, but she'd been wrong. Now he was leaving and she wouldn't see him again. The emotions he'd stirred up could be laid to rest for good.

Deep in her own thoughts, she barely noticed that Luke hadn't moved toward the door. When she did, she gave him a questioning look. "Is there something else?"

He tilted his head and glanced away from her then back. He rocked slightly on his heels.

"Luke…?"

"There's something else I need to tell you, Carly."

CHAPTER FIVE

"So, TELL ME," Carly said, studying Luke's solemn face.

"At my aunt and uncle's barbecue, I mentioned buying property. I bought the property next door."

"Next door?" Carly frowned. "Next to Tom and Frances? Are you going into the cattle business?"

"No, next door to you."

"What?" She stared at him, not quite able to take in what he was saying. "You can't mean the Withers place?" She jerked a thumb in that direction. "Why?"

"It has certain…aspects I need."

"Aspects? You mean rocks? There're plenty of those next door. But I've got news for you—there's no door, or anything else over there. Not even a shed or a shack where you could *hang* a door."

"Um, I know."

"Why on earth would you want it?" She rubbed her forehead, trying to make sense of this. "The soil's so poor and rocky a goat couldn't survive on it. You can't grow grass on it to graze cattle. The only thing that place has going for it is the stream that empties onto my land, right below my apple trees, which has long since brought most of the top-soil with it." She held her hands up, shoulder height. "And if this rain keeps up, I'll have the rest of the topsoil by July. That's why Martin Withers couldn't sell the place after his dad died and the county condemned the house and outbuildings. It's worthless."

"Not completely."

"Yes, completely, unless…" She paused, trying to remember what someone had mentioned recently about the land. "Except I heard there was an offer from someone who wanted it for—"

"My uncle bought it."

"Tom? I thought it was purchased by a group of hunters looking for private land to hunt deer and birds."

"They were interested, but Tom bought it for the same reason and sold it to me."

Now Carly's mouth dropped open. None of this made sense. "For hunting? Since when did you become a hunter? You never shot a gun, except at a carnival. You never wanted to kill anything. People change, Luke, but I can't believe you changed that much."

Luke shook his head. "I didn't, Carly. I haven't. I'm not interested in hunting or in topsoil. I'm not a farmer. I've got another project in mind."

"Another project? What kind? I'm telling you, nothing can grow there. It's only shale and…"

Eyes wide, her face draining of color, she stared at him. "Is that it? The shale?"

"Yes."

Horrifying thoughts turned over and over in her mind. "For fracturing shale to get out the oil? Fracking? Luke, you can't do that. You must know about all the problems it's caused. Besides, it's never been considered worthwhile in this part of Reston County."

"I do, but—"

"Earthquakes, polluted water." She threw her hands wide. "My place is downstream from you. I use well water on my plants. It will ruin my gardens, my apple trees. My livelihood. This is an organic garden, Luke. I've worked hard to get it established. Do you have any idea how many tons of topsoil I've bought, hauled and spread? It's taken me years to get this place established. This could ruin me."

"I know that, Carly. I'm not trying to ruin your land."

"Oh, it could simply be an unintended consequence? That makes me feel a *whole* lot better."

"Carly, calm down. It's not like that."

Panic pushed at her as her mind conjured images of parched crops and blackened fields. Breathing hard, she tried to get her rage and disappointment under control. "If it's not fracking to get out the natural gas, what is it?"

"It's another extraction method that's being developed. I'm afraid that's all I can tell you right now. The scientist I'm working with, Dr. Shelby Wayne, is keeping it under wraps because previous ideas and processes have been stolen."

"Is this so-far secret method as harmful as fracking?"

"Dr. Wayne has run endless computer models factoring in every possibility, and she assures me it's safe. But, to tell you the truth, we haven't done extensive tests yet."

"And what about the aftermath of extracting oil? All the polluted water that has to be injected deep into the substrata, where it causes earthquakes?"

"I know that, Carly. We're trying to develop a process that will avoid that."

"You're trying, but you don't *know* your so-far imaginary process will avoid those consequences? You've run computer models but you haven't done tests? So you could ruin my land, anyway, for…for old times' sake?"

"Of course not."

"Then for an experiment. Why, Luke? Why here? Why now?"

"To stop an actual fracking operation."

"What? Like I said, it hasn't been considered worthwhile to extract oil and natural gas in this part of Reston County. Who is—"

"My father."

Carly shook her head, trying to clear her increasing confusion. "Your dad? When did he get into the natural gas business? I thought he was in real estate development." She looked up. "I thought *you* were in real estate development. In Dallas. In fact, when we drove to Toncaville today, you made it sound like you're still a carpenter. Did you deliberately try to fool me? Were you laughing at me the whole time?"

"Of course not, Carly. I wouldn't do that."

"Then why didn't you tell me sooner? Was that what the ride into Toncaville was all about? Bragging about my produce, helping me rescue tortoises?"

"You invited me, remember?" He pointed to Wendolin's hope chest. "I'd honestly forgotten about the letter."

"But if you've known about this project for any amount of time, you could have phoned me. Why didn't you warn me, Luke?"

"Because I was trying to talk my dad out of this—"

"So you could do it yourself? Play at being the big energy producer? Do you see yourself as the mighty oilman on the white horse, riding in to rescue the local oil industry before it disappears completely? Rescuing it would be a great thing if it didn't involve fracking."

"*No,* Carly. I'm exactly what I've been for years—an employee of Sanderson Enterprises."

"Oh, I think you're probably more than that." She clapped her hands onto her hips. "You are Robert's son, after all."

"Try to put that aside for now. As far as real estate development is concerned, that was—*is*—our main interest. My dad invested in an exploratory energy company years ago, but nothing came of it until the past couple of years when it started paying off."

"By ruining people's property, land and water. Unbelievable." She turned away from him and paced around the living room, coming back to face him.

"Some people would argue that it means jobs in economically depressed areas like Reston County," he said.

"Those people probably aren't farmers with land to protect." Her lips trembled and furious tears formed in her eyes. "I'll fight you on this, Luke. I'll take you to court, and—"

"It wouldn't do any good, Carly. You wouldn't have a case."

Carly stuck out her chin and narrowed her eyes at him, throwing in a quick head-to-toe assessment so he'd know how enraged she was. "Oh, really? And why not?"

His face was grim as he said, "Because Sanderson Enterprises owns the mineral rights to your land. Legally, we can put a well or a fracking operation wherever we need to. It's possible that we'll find gas on my land, but it might be easier and more efficient to drill on your land and run it over to the well we'll dig on mine. We're just not sure yet.

"I know that sounds harsh, Carly, but I'm trying to be honest here, tell you exactly what could happen."

"No." Carly's legs began to shake. Luke seemed to see the depth of her distress and leaped forward to take her arm. She fought him, jerking from his grasp. She backed up until she felt the sofa behind her knees and she collapsed onto it. Her breath came in gasps as she said, "No, Luke. That's not possible. This is our land. My parents bought it fifteen years ago from…"

"My dad." Luke turned and moved away, taking the chair opposite her. He sat, leaning forward, his hands on his knees as he watched her reactions. "He'd owned it for a few years, but when he decided to sell, he gave your parents a bargain price in exchange for letting him retain the mineral rights. And… I'm sure my dad drove a hard bargain—generous on the one hand and relentless on the other."

"They wouldn't have done that, Luke!"

"But they did. They probably never thought the mineral rights would be worth anything. No one around here did. And they weren't worth anything for many years, but it's different now."

"Yeah, and obviously Robert Sanderson knew."

"It's the way he's always done business. The way he grew up. The way his family did business. It was common practice to sell the land but retain the mineral rights. It's the same way here. You must know that, Carly."

She did, but she'd never thought it would apply to her, to her land. Why hadn't her parents told her? For that matter, why hadn't Tom and Frances told her? She'd thought they were her friends.

She felt sick. Betrayed all around.

"And now he's taking advantage of those mineral rights. How many other pieces of land has he ruined? Have you helped him ruin?"

"None!"

"As far as you know."

He shook his head in frustration. "I can't answer that or give you any facts I don't have."

"From what you've said so far, you wouldn't tell me even if you did know."

Before he could answer she threw her hands in the air. "Never mind. This is a pointless... merry-go-round. Nightmare-go-round," she amended. "It's time for you to go, Luke, and... and don't come back."

"Carly, if you'd listen to me, I can at least tell you—"

"Lies?" She held up her hand. "No." Her sense of anger and betrayal made it impossible for her to go on with this conversation. "Go."

As if to emphasize her fury, the windows

rattled in their frames and the ceiling fan rocked back and forth.

"Earthquake," she said accusingly, as if merely talking about oil extraction had caused it.

"Well, it's not my fault."

"Yet."

Luke swung toward the door. "I'll be back in three months and then you'll have to listen to me."

"Don't count on it."

In a swirl of emotions, she watched him stride across the yard, climb into his truck and drive away.

He couldn't do this. There had to be a way to stop this catastrophe from happening. She stood, paced around the living room and tried to focus. Finally a moment of clarity surfaced.

"Lisa," she said out loud. Lisa was in real estate. She would know what to do.

SHAKEN AND SICK at heart, Luke drove away from Joslin Gardens. He'd done it again, hurt her when he hadn't meant to. He'd stumbled around, tripping over his good intentions, and landed face-first in a disaster. He pounded his fist on the steering wheel. If only she'd listened to him, let him explain how this had come about, but she'd been too angry and upset to hear what he had to say.

She was right. He should have told her as soon as he finalized the deal with Tom to buy the old Withers place. Reasons and excuses ran through his mind. Because he'd spent the entire drive from Dallas stewing over delivering the trunk and seeing Carly again, he'd thought he was ready to handle everything in a businesslike manner.

Not even close. He'd been thrown off-kilter when he'd seen her, struck by her strength and beauty, the success she'd made of the gardens her parents had struggled to establish.

He'd slipped into some fantasy world where the two of them would be friends, neighbors for a time, and the past would be forgotten. If he'd been thinking clearly, he would have done the right thing and told her straightaway. He only had himself to blame.

He would give her time to calm down and then try again, or maybe call Gemma Whitmire or Lisa Thomas and ask their advice.

"Yeah, right," he muttered. "They'll give

me advice, all right, by telling me exactly where to go."

For the next three months he would be tied up in Dallas before he could move up here and be on-site for the development of the new process—practically on Carly's doorstep. She would have to listen to him then.

Distracted by his thoughts and annoyed with himself, Luke rounded a curve a mile from Joslin Gardens and slammed on his brakes to avoid a skinny boy on a beat-up, overloaded bicycle. Although he was riding at the edge of the road, there wasn't much room on the narrow highway. Boxes were attached on the front and back of the bike, and they appeared to be loaded with greenery. Glancing around to make sure there wasn't any traffic, he pulled up beside the kid and put down his window. The boy gave him a suspicious glance but kept on pedaling.

Driving at a snail's pace to stay alongside, Luke called out, "Hey, buddy, can I give you a ride into town?"

The boy looked over and shook his head. "No, thanks. I'm okay." As if he couldn't help himself, he lifted his arm and wiped his sweaty face on the sleeve of his T-shirt. His raggedly cut dark hair stood on end and he left a streak of dirt across his cheek.

"I'm going that way. Might as well make it easy on yourself."

"Nah. This is easy enough." Even as he said it, his front wheel wobbled and his thin legs shook with the effort of climbing a small rise.

"Riding in my air-conditioned truck would make it a whole lot easier. And I've got some water."

Luke viewed his own persistence sardonically. He knew exactly why he was doing this. His failure with Carly was pushing him to do at least *one* thing right today. This reluctant boy happened to be in the path of his good intentions.

The boy paused and then stopped, licking his dry lips. The mention of water had caught his attention, but he narrowed his big, brown eyes. "You won't try anything funny, will ya?"

Luke swallowed a laugh while appearing to take the boy's question seriously. "No, I promise. I'll even let you hold my cell phone the whole way into town in case you want to call the sheriff for help."

"I ain't calling the sheriff." He considered the offer for a few more seconds. He studied the pickup and then Luke's face. "Okay, then." The words seemed to be dragged out of him. "Just to the middle of town." He nodded toward the full boxes. "I've got some stuff to sell."

"Do you think you'll need a license?" Luke asked, half-jokingly.

The boy smirked. "I'm a kid. Who's gonna hassle a kid for selling stuff?"

Obviously this was a street-smart boy, Luke thought as he set his hazard lights to flashing and got out to help load the bike and boxes into the back of his truck.

It took a couple of minutes to unfasten the boxes, which had been attached to the frame with a clever arrangement of boards and rusted wire. Luke couldn't even see exactly what the boy planned to sell because the boxes were so full of leaves.

When they finished, Luke opened the truck door and held it while the boy climbed inside. "My name's Luke Sanderson. What's yours?"

The kid treated him to another suspicious look as he fastened his seat belt. "Dustin."

Luke slammed the door and walked around the front to climb behind the wheel once again. As promised, he handed over his cell phone, which made the boy blink in surprise, but he took it.

Luke reached behind the front seat to grab a bottle of water, which he handed to Dustin. This time, there was no argument as he twisted off the cap and gulped the cool drink.

"Thanks, mister," he mumbled.

"Do you live around here?" Luke asked.

"Yeah."

Luke gave the boy a curious glance. "Have you got a last name?"

"Dustin's enough," he said.

Luke took the hint and didn't ask any more questions, but he couldn't help speculating. He couldn't tell his age—anywhere between ten and thirteen—but he seemed small for whatever age he was. Other than being unkempt, Dustin appeared to be healthy enough—if somewhat underfed.

They finished the ride into Reston in silence and Luke dropped the boy off in front of one of the supermarkets, along with his bike and boxes. Dustin returned the cell phone, gave a wave of thanks and wheeled his bike around back. Luke continued on his way, his thoughts equally divided between Carly and the ragged boy he'd just met.

Say what she would, Carly had to understand that people needed jobs in this area, families deserved more and better resources than what were currently available. He had no idea what Dustin's story was since the boy hadn't been much of a talker, but it was obvious he had needs that weren't being met. Luke decided he would tell Frances about the boy. If anyone could help, it was his aunt.

"I DON'T SEE that you have any alternative, Carly." Lisa looked up from the deed they'd found on file at the county courthouse.

Carly had called her parents, who had confirmed that Robert Sanderson had retained the mineral rights. They had apologized for not telling her sooner, but, at the time, they were so thrilled at the bargain they were getting, they'd never thought mineral rights would be an issue.

Now Carly and Lisa sat side by side at an ancient, polished table in the conference room of the hundred-year-old red-rock building, reading every word of the deed while dust motes swirled in the sunlight streaming through the window.

"You mean I have to let them go ahead with this project—whatever it is?"

Lisa lifted one perfectly sculpted eyebrow at her. "If you hadn't blown up at Luke, you would probably *know* what this project entails."

"Maybe."

"Certainly."

Carly flopped back against her chair. "Lisa, *he* didn't even seem to know. It appears that he's backing a scientist. I'm guessing he's a petroleum engineer, who's got an untried, untested process in the works."

"He must know something about it, Carly, or he wouldn't be putting money into it."

"Yeah, you're right." Troubled, Carly put her elbow on the armrest and propped up her head with her palm while she considered everything she'd learned from Luke, which wasn't much. "He believes in this Dr.

Wayne, which means this scientist has done something in the past worth believing in. But I don't think Luke would blindly hand out money without some kind of guarantee of a return on his investment."

"That's probably true," Lisa answered, thinking it over. "He is Robert's son, after all."

"Don't remind me. Or yourself."

Lisa went back to examining the deed and Carly sighed. Lisa was right. She'd been in the real estate business for ten years, working hard to establish her reputation and secure the type of financial security she hadn't known when they were growing up. She had a head for figures, was smart with money and was bone-deep honest. Any advice Lisa gave would be carefully considered—even if it wasn't what Carly wanted to hear.

"But I can file a lawsuit or get an injunction or something, right?"

"It wouldn't hurt to talk to an attorney, but filing lawsuits and injunctions costs money, which you should probably save for an emergency."

Distressed and exhausted from the roller

coaster of emotions she'd been through that day, Carly dropped her forehead into her hand. "In case my garden is ruined and I have to live in my truck—or the back of my Upcycle shop."

"On which you haven't even signed a lease yet," Lisa pointed out, returning the deed to its folder.

"But what if...?"

Lisa placed her hands on top of the folder and tapped her fingers. "Enough with the ifs, Carly. As hard as you work, there's no possibility that the shop will fail, and its success will be another income stream for you, better than the one you've got now with your helter-skelter approach to selling the pieces you've renovated."

"Helter-skelter?"

"You know it's true. That's why you've got a barnful—"

"Not a barn," Carly interrupted. "More of a large shed."

Lisa ignored the interruption. "Of refurbished pieces sitting and gathering dust. Hoarding them won't bring you any money."

"I'm not hoarding."

Lisa gave her a level stare. "Carly, remember my grandparents? The house I grew up in? They didn't start out as hoarders but they ended up that way because they couldn't part with anything. Why keep all the pieces you've redone when you could sell them and earn money?"

"Which I'll need."

"My point exactly." Lisa returned the folder to the clerk then said, "It doesn't do you any good to borrow trouble. Whatever Luke is planning is going to happen whether you get hysterical about it or not, but it'll be a lot easier on you if you calm down and focus on the things you *can* control—like your two businesses."

Begrudgingly, Carly stood and followed her. "I hate it when you're right."

"I know," Lisa answered in a satisfied tone.

"Let's go look at that shop space on Main Street again. I'm pretty sure that's the one I want. It's got a covered area out back that would be perfect for renovating my stock. I can hire and train someone to help me, maybe a couple of people."

"Now you're talking. Between the gardens and the shop, you'll be providing jobs."

"I know, and that's something near and dear to your heart."

"Of course. It's my hometown. We need more employment here."

"Luke claims his project will create jobs—along with pollution and habitat destruction."

"You don't know that yet, and I doubt Luke said it," Lisa cautioned.

"Are you defending him? Whose side are you on, anyway?"

Lisa's eyes widened with hurt. "Carly! We've been best friends since we were babies. How can you ask whose side I'm on?"

Carly glanced away. "I'm sorry. I'm hurt, angry and confused."

"Which is why you need to talk to an attorney." Lisa smiled gently. "I'm not choosing sides, I'm telling you that you don't need to borrow trouble."

Carly nodded glumly. "Yeah, I'll sit around and wait for it to come find me."

Lisa put her arm around her and gave a squeeze. "I'll call Gemma and get her to stop for a bottle of sparkling cider and meet us at your new business. We'll have a toast."

"Tell her to get a pizza, too. I'm hungry."

Lisa laughed and made the call. When she hung up, she said, "Pizza is our only fast-food option in this town. We need some fast-casual outfits, not junk food, but healthy, delicious alternatives—who could be customers for Joslin Gardens."

"If I'm still in business." She waved her hands as if she had a magician's wand. "Well, start looking into it, Lisa. You found a buyer for the Mustang Supermarket and got it re-opened. I'll bet you could get some food trucks, or a falafel stand, to come to Reston."

"Don't mock. I just might do that."

They stepped outside, where they were hit by a gust of wind and a sprinkle of rain.

"More rain," Carly said, dismayed. "My fields haven't even dried out from the last storm. Some of my plants are developing leaf rot."

"You must have known another one was coming. You study the weather report like someone's going to give you an exam."

"I know, but I wanted to go back to Toncaville and take a swing through the resale shops, see what I can find to renovate."

"No. As I said not three minutes ago, you've got plenty of stock for now. You're simply terrified of not being busy enough." Lisa dashed toward the parking lot. "Come on."

Carly watched her and sighed. Lisa was the only person she knew who could jump puddles and run between raindrops while wearing a formfitting dress and four-inch heels. That made her think of Frances Sanderson's story about somersaulting down the staircase at the prom. She was still deeply troubled by the fact that they'd known about Luke's plans and hadn't told her.

She could call Frances and ask her. Or maybe she could call Luke and talk to him in a calm, rational manner, learn all the facts without getting upset.

"Well, not yet," she murmured, heading for her truck. She was a long way from being rational about this.

CHAPTER SIX

THE OVERWHELMING SPRING rains relented by the end of June and the summer passed with hot, steamy days and humid nights that seemed to make the season drag on forever. Joslin Gardens prospered, but Carly, Jay and Sheena spent days reinforcing fence posts loosened by the rain and harvesting the rapidly maturing produce.

Carly hired more help in the gardens, and was at last able to open Upcycle in early fall. The two employees she found for the shop had previous retail experience so she felt confident they could handle her new venture.

She met with an attorney who confirmed what Lisa had said. She needed to wait and see what Luke was going to do. She couldn't stop him from extracting natural gas from shale on his own land, and since Sanderson Enterprises owned the mineral rights to hers, he could drill on her property, too. She was, by turns, frustrated, angry and curious.

It didn't help that she'd seen him briefly at one of the hospital fund-raisers, an ice-cream social organized by his aunt Frances. He'd said they were in the planning stages and he couldn't tell her anything yet. She'd stalked away in fury.

As hard as she worked, and as busy as she kept herself, Luke and his impending project were never far from her mind, especially when the gentle stream that crossed the old Withers place and emptied onto her land turned into a raging creek. It picked up debris from the derelict land and sent it crashing against her cedar fence posts, slackening their grip in the soil so that they tilted sideways. A few had collapsed all the way to the ground. Carly feared the gaps would be an open invitation to wildlife or even stray cattle if the Sandersons decided to start raising beef along with their real estate and oil businesses.

The rushing water had also loosened the soil around some of her smaller apple trees and one day, when they had a little time, she and Jay went out to survey the damage.

"At least the water has gone down," Jay observed, walking up the bank to the drunken-looking fence and gazing at the neighboring property.

"And this streambed looks like it's been scrubbed out with a giant wire brush." Dismayed, Carly studied the broken branches, torn-out bushes and exposed rock. She had never expected this much rain to fall in a few short weeks or for so much of her precious topsoil to have been stripped away. Most people would have seen that as a concern, but to her, it was also a lost investment and environmental hazard. She glanced down at the now innocent-looking stream. She had been in the organic gardening business for twelve years, but she had never experienced anything like this.

"I think I can fix these posts, Carly," Jay said. "But I've got some things to do for my dad every day after school so I probably can't get to it until Sunday afternoon."

"Okay. We'll look at it then and see what needs to be done. We may have to go into town for supplies," she answered, distracted by the erosion pattern. The water had flooded over from the land on which Luke would be trying out his mysterious new process, only increasing her worries about runoff ruining her gardens.

"Do you think animals will get in if the fence is down," Jay asked. "Wild hogs and stuff?"

"I don't know," Carly said. "Why? Do you see tracks?"

"Not yet, but it probably won't be long before we see evidence of their little pig feet." He nodded toward the Withers place. "And once they start building over there, all the wildlife will be looking for new homes."

"I know."

"What do you think it is they're going to be doing, Carly?"

"I wish I knew."

Jay found the entire operation fascinating and reported back to her on every new piece of equipment that was trucked over the adjoining property's recently resurfaced drive and around to the back of a hill, out of sight.

Carly knew she should stop him, but not a word of information about the project had been released and she was wildly curious.

"Yesterday they hauled in a mobile office," Jay announced as they turned back toward their four-wheeler.

"A mobile office?"

"You know, the kind you see at construction sites."

"Oh?" Carly looked at him curiously as she slipped behind the wheel and headed home.

"And this morning somebody drove in a motor home—a big, fancy one pulling a trailer with an old VW Bug on it. It's still there."

"Did you see who was driving it?"

Jay shrugged. "Some lady."

Deep in her thoughts about possible runoff, she didn't realize what he'd said at first. "Wait, Jay. The new road goes all the way around on the other side of the hill. How have you seen what they've been hauling in?"

He avoided her gaze. "Oh, I may have seen someone up there in the woods, and I may have kinda gone to take a little look."

She raised an eyebrow at him. "You *may* have seen someone in the woods? Did it occur to you that it might be someone who actually works over there? Someone Luke hired?"

"Sure." Jay gave her an insulted look. "But if he was supposed to be there, why was he sneaking around?"

"What do you mean, exactly, by 'sneaking around'?"

"I think it's self-explanatory. Running from one tree to another and hiding behind them, trying not to be seen. I didn't get a good look at him so I tried to get closer."

"And did it work?"

"No, whoever it was disappeared..."

"But by that time, you were trespassing."

"Yeah, I guess."

"Jay, I'm serious. I don't want to have a conflict with the Sandersons. You know I was once married to Luke, right?"

"Well, yeah." He frowned and bit his lip.

"In spite of that, I don't know him, don't really know who he is now or what he's doing."

The sense of anger and betrayal was strong and it extended to Frances and Tom. They had said they were sorry she was hurt, but they'd felt it was Luke's place to tell her about his plans for the land.

"So, you guys aren't friends, huh?" Jay asked.

She laughed softly. "And never will be."

Carly stopped the four-wheeler in front of the shed and stepped out of the vehicle. "I don't want any trouble with whatever Sanderson Enterprises has going on over there, so please don't go on their land."

Jay frowned. "Okay, but there's something funny going on."

"Yes, I know. My gardens are under threat, and you might get arrested for trespassing."

"No, there's something else going on. I know I saw someone sneaking around over there. Remember when I told you the blueberries seemed to be disappearing?"

"Yes, but that was months ago, before any of the Sanderson people arrived."

"Well, okay," Jay acknowledged. "Then it can't be them. But other things have disappeared, too. I thought it was animals, but now I'm beginning to wonder."

"What kinds of things?"

"Come on, I'll show you."

Jay led the way into the field where the pole beans had been staked. The spring's soggy soil had delayed the full production of the crop, but they were growing well now and Carly hoped to have a full harvest before the first frost. Luck hadn't been on her side this year, but she was ever hopeful of a change for the better.

"Did you pick these?" he asked, pointing to the sparse number of pods on one pole about halfway down the row. "I know I didn't, and Sheena said she didn't, either."

"No." Carly looked at the plants on either side. "These are full. So what happened?"

Jay's eyes lit with triumph. He crossed his arms over his chest and said, "Somebody's been stealing our produce."

"Stealing it?" Carly examined the ground around the pole, reaching down to push foliage out of the way. "I don't see any tracks or evidence of anyone having been here. Maybe it's like you said, wild animals."

"Might be, but wouldn't they leave tracks? And look at this."

She followed him a couple of rows over to where carrots were growing, their feathery tops bending in the gentle breeze. "About every third carrot is missing." He crossed his arms and nodded as if that was the last word on the subject.

Carly swallowed a giggle. "You counted them?"

"Nah, but they're farther apart than they were before, not spaced evenly the way you like them, and I don't think some of them jumped up and ran away."

"Again, if it was animals, wouldn't we be seeing tracks?" she asked, pointing to the soft, unmarred dirt.

"If it was anything, or *anybody*, wouldn't we be seeing tracks?" he countered.

"Yes, of course." She paused. "And you think you saw somebody over on the old Withers place?"

"Yeah, I did. I'm sure of it." His young face set in determination. "And I'm going to find out who it is, too."

Carly considered him for a moment. He was really taking the initiative on this, which would be a good learning experience for him. On the other hand, she wasn't paying him to track down thieves who really weren't doing much damage. When she saw his eager look, though, she knew she couldn't dampen his enthusiasm. "Just don't trespass."

Jay answered with a long-suffering sigh

but then nodded. He crouched, examining the ground like a detective on the trail of a criminal while Carly grinned to herself and headed for the truck. She had packed it with her most recent refurbished stock and was ready to deliver it to Upcycle.

While it was true that she couldn't afford to lose produce, especially in a year when so much of her crop had been delayed by wet weather, she had too many other things on her mind right now to worry about disappearing beans and walking carrots.

Back inside her house, she picked up a few things she needed to take with her, but as she passed through the living room her attention was caught by Wendolin's statue and she stopped to pick it up.

She had held and admired it dozens of times since Luke had brought it to her. The perfection of the tiny girl's features amazed her and every time she looked at it, she marveled at the artist's skill. Carly was sure she could see the face of the elderly woman she had loved in the figure's flawless features. She thought back over every conversation she'd had with Wendolin, all the times she'd fled to her house when trying to be a city dweller, the urban wife she knew she wasn't.

"Talking is the only solution," Wendolin often said in her softly accented voice.

But it hadn't been the solution for her and Luke. At least, not then. Neither of them had been able to say the right things.

Reaching into her pocket, she pulled out her cell phone. She had his number and she'd called him once after seeing him at the ice-cream social. It had been cut short because he'd had to go to a meeting. When he'd called back, they were being hit by an electrical storm, so she hadn't found the answers she needed that day.

Carly knew she could have contacted him again, *should* have contacted him again, in spite of the attorney's advice to wait and see what would happen, but she had put it off. Glancing at the clock, she found an excuse to delay it again. She had to get this load of goods into Upcycle so that her employees, Janie and Troy, could help her arrange everything.

Her shop had been open for a few days, but the grand opening was still to come—

organized by Lisa and doubtless assisted by Gemma…as soon as she returned from her honeymoon.

Carly gave Sheena instructions on what needed to be done before she left that afternoon, then started toward town. She stopped at the hardware store for some heavy-duty shelf brackets to reinforce some shelves in Upcycle's back room.

When she walked outside, she had to step back quickly to avoid a kid on an ancient bicycle. He was riding, head down, along the edge of the street while struggling to balance a box on the front of his bike.

"Oh, be careful," she said, but he didn't respond, pedaling hard as he turned into the parking lot of the Mustang Supermarket.

Carly stared after him, sure she'd never seen him before, but she wondered why he wasn't in school at this hour.

With a shrug, she continued to her shop where she and her employees unloaded and arranged as much as they could, then stored the remainder of the stock in the back room. Janie and Troy went for a late lunch, leaving Carly to walk around the shop, tweaking a few items. As she did, Lisa walked in with a lunch bag and a to-go cup of sweet iced tea.

"I'm guessing you haven't eaten lunch yet," Lisa said, handing the items over and glancing at the clock, which indicated it was after two thirty.

"You're right," Carly answered, gratefully accepting the food. "I'm famished." She grinned at Lisa. "Even if I had eaten, though, I'd still be hungry."

"I know," Lisa said on a sigh. "I had lettuce leaves for lunch."

While Carly scrubbed her hands and then ate the sandwich, Lisa wandered around and commented on the items Carly had beautified with her artistic touch.

"I remember when you got this chair," she said, giving the cream-colored gliding rocker a gentle push. Carly had painted red and yellow roses on the headrest and down the arms. She'd accented it with red cushions. "It was in a hundred pieces."

"At least," Carly agreed. "It was like putting together a jigsaw puzzle."

Eyes narrowed, Lisa gave her a speculative look. "How many hours did it take you to finish it?"

"Altogether, about ten or twelve over a few days."

"And you're asking $69.95 for it."

"So?" Carly eyed her warily. Whenever Lisa had this expression on her face, it usually meant she had an idea brewing.

"That's not even minimum wage. You need to be asking more for your pieces. This is beautiful. It's a work of art."

"Look around, Lisa. This isn't the big city where rich folks will come strolling in and spend huge amounts on furniture."

"Which is why you need to advertise. You need to jazz up your website so it features everything you have for sale."

"That sounds like a lot of work." Carly finished the last bite of her sandwich, tossed the bag in the trash and sipped her tea.

"You can hire one of the kids from the tech class at the high school. Owen Forester, for example, could probably add some pizzazz to your site in no time and keep it updated. He's only fifteen so he'll be around for a while to help you out. And, besides, when have *you* ever been afraid of hard work?"

"This is different. I'm already learning more than I ever thought I would need to know about the retail business. I know I've got trustworthy people covering the gardens, but it's going to be a huge job to keep up the stock here, almost like having a single job again, at least for a while, and I haven't done that…" She paused, thinking back. "Since I saw how much Wendolin got accomplished by working at different jobs rather than focusing on one until it was completed, like I'd always been taught. Funny, I never made that connection before."

"You learned a lot from her."

"Yes. She also taught me how to do needlepoint."

"Except that you never sit down long enough to actually finish any needlepoint."

"It's in my long-range plan."

"This is going to be an outstanding success," Lisa stated in a no-nonsense tone.

Janie and Troy returned right then, so Lisa picked up Carly's iced tea and tugged her into the back room.

"What are you doing?" Carly asked, looking around. "You don't want to be in here. You're way too much of a princess."

"Remember how I grew up, Carly. I've earned my princessness."

"Is that even a word?"

"I'm willing to take a chance on getting dusty. Sit," Lisa ordered, pointing to one of the many chairs crowding the workroom. Then she dusted off one for herself and perched on it.

"Carly, I understood—Gemma and I both understood—that you were afraid to start this business right now."

"But I'm doing it, aren't I?" Carly asked, throwing her arms out. "This is what you both thought I should do."

"And it's still a good idea, but you're so worried and stressed about the situation with Luke and his mysterious project, I'm afraid you're not going to get any pleasure out of it."

Carly set her cup down on a nearby cabinet and shook her head. "It isn't only the project, it's the fact that he, his dad actually, owns the mineral rights to my property. I hate standing on my land and knowing my family only owns the top few inches, that the rest belongs to someone who doesn't care about it. I hate knowing that he could do anything and I would have no say in it."

"Do you think Luke would do that?"

"No. I'm not sure," she amended. "I don't know him anymore. He's not the man I knew, but I suspect Robert is still the same."

"I'm sure Luke's changed. You've changed, too, for that matter. The only way you're going to get an answer is to call Luke, ask him when the project will start and what it will involve."

"I already know it's going to involve masses of heavy equipment…and destruction."

Lisa shook her head again. She picked up the slim clutch that matched her green high-heeled pumps. They even had green butterflies embroidered on the vamps. "I've got to show a piece of property this afternoon, so I'll say only one more thing. You need to call Luke, get all the information you need—or at least any he can share. I wish Gemma was here to back me up, but she's not, so I'll go it alone.

"Carly, you've worked hard for twelve years to turn yourself into the person you are now. You always get the answers you need and you don't leave anything to chance." Lisa walked over and gave her a hug. "You've stalled long enough."

Until today, Carly thought as Lisa walked out. She was right, and again, Carly heard Wendolin's soft voice reminding her that matters could be solved by talking. In spite of the reluctance that dragged at her, the memory of the destruction caused by the flooded stream had her punching Luke's number and waiting for him to answer.

"Hello? This is Luke."

At the sound of his voice, she shivered. A faint echo told her she was on speakerphone. "Um, yes, Luke. It's Carly. I want to ask you about what's going on. There are masses of equipment on the Withers place and I'm wondering exactly what's going to be happening and when it's going to happen."

She heard a click and the echo disappeared. "I'm not sure yet, Carly. We'll be starting in the next couple of weeks, though. Almost all of the equipment has arrived and Dr. Wayne is on-site."

"Starting soon, hmm?" she asked then told him about the rain and the destruction it had caused in the stream and some of the surrounding area.

"I can't have my gardens destroyed, Luke. Not after all the work I've… People depend on my produce." Carly paused, hating that her voice was shaking. She took a deep breath and asked, "What can you tell me?"

"Not much, I'm afraid. At least, not about the process. I'm sorry there's not more to tell, but I promise I'll do everything I can to avoid harm to your property or business."

She paused again, thinking about it. "I guess that's the best I can ask for. At least for now. Goodbye, Luke." Discouraged, she hung up, dropped her cell phone into her pocket and chose a polishing rag from a pile on the counter. Dipping one corner into a can of paste wax, she set to work.

"You don't have to apologize, you know," Robert Sanderson said from where he stood by the door. "It's just business."

Luke shook his head. "It's more than that, Dad, and we both know it. I've asked before, but I never got an answer. Why start an extraction process in Reston County now? You could have started it anytime since you sold that property all those years ago. Those rights were always yours."

"The time wasn't right."

Luke frowned at his father. Robert had always been a driven man, but he showed no signs of slowing down, despite being well into his sixties and having high blood pressure that required three different medications.

"What makes the time right now, Dad?"

But Robert gave the same unsatisfying answer he always did. "Funding, interest, siting the operation where jobs are needed."

"People don't need their community destroyed. Carly doesn't need her land destroyed."

"That wasn't my plan."

"No, but if I hadn't jumped on the property and bought it from Tom, you would have bought it and exercised your rights to the minerals on her property."

Robert gave a skeptical laugh. "Isn't that what you're doing?"

"I'm hoping not to."

"Ask any geologist or petroleum engineer. Pockets of natural gas aren't always where indications say they will be. You might have to drill on her land."

"I know, Dad. And I've told her that."

Robert's frown only deepened. "Yeah, I guess you have to be in communication with her." He paused, thinking it over, and Luke wondered what was really going through his father's mind.

Finally, Robert went on. "But believe me when I tell you, people worry a lot less about that in places like Reston, especially when they're so slow to recover from the recession. You'll see." Robert looked a bit smug when he said it. "If this fairy-tale fracking process of yours comes true, you'll see exactly what I mean."

"It isn't a fairy tale, Dad, as you well know."

Robert shrugged. "Whatever it is, the calendar is counting down. You've only got nine months from the finalization of the land purchase to prove this process works, and then it's all mine."

Luke rubbed the space between his eyes,

where a headache was starting. "I know, Dad. I know. But why nine months?"

"Because six is too short and a year is too long to wait and see if this is going to pay off."

His dad's focus was always the bottom line.

"All right. Nine months it is."

Robert looked at Luke for a few seconds longer then turned and left. Luke got back to the projects he needed to deal with before he left Dallas but was interrupted when his secretary announced two visitors. A Ms. Thomas and a Ms. Whitmire.

Luke stared at the intercom. "You're kidding."

"Um, no, sir. Those are their names."

"I'll be right there." He hurried to the door and threw it open to find Carly Joslin's two best friends standing by his secretary's desk. They were dressed for the occasion—whatever it was—in tailored dresses and high heels.

"Hello," he said, trying for a friendly tone. But they were all business. As soon as he swung the door wide, they marched inside.

"Have a seat," he invited. "What brings you to Dallas?"

"We won't be here long enough to sit down," Lisa said crisply.

"And you're what brought us to Dallas," Gemma added.

He studied their determined expressions. "I'm guessing this isn't about my oil and gas extraction process."

"You'd be right," Lisa answered. "It's about Carly. From what we hear, you don't know how long you'll be in Reston."

"That's right."

"We just want you to know that while you're there, we'll be watching you so that you don't hurt Carly again," Gemma said. She possessed the no-nonsense attitude of a nurse who had dealt with difficult situations. Right now, *he* was the difficult situation.

"I wasn't planning on it."

"I'm sure you didn't plan on it the last time, either, but that's how it worked out." Lisa looked him up and down as if he was a piece of real estate in need of a complete teardown.

He couldn't deny what she said. It echoed his own guilty thoughts.

"So do we have your promise?"

They both crossed their arms and waited

for him to answer. He knew they wouldn't leave until they got what they came for. He would laugh if this wasn't so crazy.

"I promise I will do everything in my power to keep from hurting Carly again."

"Good." Lisa nodded at Gemma. "I think our work here is done."

They turned on their heels to leave, but paused when he said, "Carly's lucky to have you two for friends."

"Just remember that." Lisa used the first two fingers of her right hand to point to her eyes and then to him in the I'll-be-watching-you gesture. They went out the door and closed it behind them with a click that echoed with purpose.

"I think I was visited by the Stiletto Mafia," he said aloud. "Guess I'd better be glad they didn't hint about cement overshoes and a quick trip to the middle of Lake Texoma."

Grinning, he went back to work.

"I THINK THE thief is some kind of animal," Sheena said. She had gone home after work, just like always, but Jay had called, so she'd rushed right back. He had *never* called her before.

She was amazed to arrive back at Carly's nearly empty shed to find him inside with various pieces of camping equipment spread out around him. Right now, she was using a hand mirror he'd borrowed from Carly's house to apply various shades of camouflage makeup to his face. It made him look even more handsome—and dangerous. Like an action hero or a Navy SEAL.

He was wearing camo shirt, pants and boots and his motorcycle helmet was nearby.

"Are those the clothes you wear hunting?" No one in her family hunted, so this was all new to her.

"Not when I'm after game," he said in a matter-of-fact tone. "Then I have to wear high-visibility reflective gear so some dumb hunter doesn't shoot me."

He seemed to like that she was asking questions. They'd never had such a personal conversation before. "You look like you're heading off to war."

"I am. Like I said, I don't think an animal

is what's been stealing Carly's produce, but if it is, we'll be eating it for breakfast."

Sheena grimaced. "If it's skunk, no thanks."

"I don't think it's skunk."

"So, you're going to lie in wait in the field and see what you can catch, right?"

"That's right."

"So why am I here?"

"You're my backup."

Her heartbeat picked up as she gave him a delighted smile. "I am? What am I supposed to do because… I can't stay out here all night. My mom would kill me."

"Nah, all you have to do is call me every couple of hours so my phone will vibrate and remind me to stay awake." Jay puffed out his chest a little. "I can stay awake if I want to, but I might need a reminder."

Sheena gave him a brilliant smile. "Well, won't that mean I'll have to stay awake all night, too?"

"Yeah. I told you, you're my backup."

"Well, okay, but can't you set your phone to vibrate every couple of hours or something?"

"Nah." He glanced away, his cheeks red. "I've got this cheapie thing of my mom's that's like a hundred years old." Jay took the old flip phone from his pocket and showed her. "All it does is make phone calls. Can't even text. But it does vibrate."

"All right, then. I'll call you, but you need to answer sometimes so I know you're okay."

"Thanks, Sheena." He gestured toward his gear. "Can you help me carry all this stuff out under the apple trees? I've got the feeling that's where this guy, or whatever it is, will hit next 'cause the apples are getting ripe. I want to bed down early and cover myself with branches and stuff—you know, like army snipers do—and be ready."

"Sure, I can do that." She hesitated. "But it's supposed to be a full moon tonight. Do you think the thief might be able to see you?"

"Sheena, I know all about camouflage and making myself invisible to the enemy."

She sighed inwardly. He was so smart. She picked up his sleeping bag and a canteen of water. It would have been nice if he was paying more attention to her than his mission, but she would take what she could get.

There was enough light left for them to make their way to the apple trees. After checking for snakes, and every other possible creature, he snuggled into his sleeping bag and, in dramatic whispers, directed Sheena on where to place the branches so he was completely covered.

When she was finished, Sheena assured him he couldn't be seen. After promising to call every two hours, she slipped away.

JAY SETTLED DOWN, making a conscious effort to listen to all the sounds around him. He was pretty sure that if he listened carefully enough, he could tell the difference between a rabbit and a field rat. He practiced math games in his head, ran through basketball plays, even replayed all the times last school year when he'd made three-pointers. He was going to stay awake—no problem.

CHAPTER SEVEN

HE SLIPPED THROUGH the leaning fence, being careful not to snag his skin or his clothes on the barbed wire. He pulled his bag through the opening, too, ready to pick the vegetables he needed for tomorrow.

A low, rumbling noise, followed by three short snuffling bursts froze him in his tracks. His heart pounding, he looked around, watching for beady little eyes glowing in the dark, but he saw nothing and there was no sound of movement. Deciding that whatever had made the noise was gone now, he lifted his foot, ready to move out.

Another rumble, then a whole series of bursts, stopped him. It was an animal. His attention fixed on a high mound of branches and twigs, he worked up the courage to step closer. Was that a bear's den? With a bear in it? If it woke up, would it eat him?

He didn't intend to find out.

At that moment, another blast of sound rumbled from the den, and it moved. A leg, and then an arm thrashed about. The leg was wearing a boot.

He grinned. Why was someone sleeping out here? Even though this was private land, it wasn't a place to hunt, and if this guy was hoping to get the jump on a rabbit or deer, it wasn't going to happen with all this snoring going on.

Picking up his bag, he started to turn away but then stopped as an idea occurred to him. Maybe this guy was out here to catch *him*, to stop him from getting what he needed. Fear raced through him for a second, but when another snore erupted, he relaxed. This guy wasn't going to wake up.

Grateful for the full moon, he dug in his pocket and pulled out a couple of items. After a few minutes he finished his preparations, grabbed his things and stole away to begin the night's harvest.

LUKE BRACED HIMSELF against the window frame as he gazed out at the Dallas skyline, glittering with lights. It was an impressive city, built on oil, commerce and cattle, but he was ready to leave it behind, at least for now.

Ever since his aunt and uncle had bought property in Reston and made themselves an integral part of the community, he'd thought about going there. Then, when he'd found out his father still owned the mineral rights to Carly's land and was looking for a new place to sink a natural gas well, he'd known he had to do something about it. Buying the land next door had been nothing short of a miracle. Finding Shelby Wayne had been another one. Convincing his dad to let him try what he hoped would be a less invasive and destructive extraction technique had completed the trifecta of victory. The problem was that, because of delays, he now had only six months to perform a miracle.

And at the same time, he planned to look for his next project or maybe even career. Although he hadn't shared that information with his dad. He had been restless ever since Omi had become ill and needed his help.

The gratitude she'd showed, her sweet thankfulness that her only grandchild was willing to take hours, even days, off from work to be with her, to take care of her, had shaken him into the realization that he was missing out on a big, important chunk of life. That's why he had taken so much time away from the office, so he could sit and talk to her, storing up her advice, her memories of his mom and of his own childhood—though she'd revealed very little of her own.

The busyness of his life had made him forget some of the things he had liked to do with his grandparents, like helping his grandfather build birdhouses and organize all the little jars of nuts, bolts and screws in the garage.

In all of their talks, though, Omi had rarely mentioned Carly or brought up their brief, disastrous marriage, except to say that at some point he needed to let go of the past. She said she'd given Carly the same advice, and that both of them worked too hard.

Omi also said he needed to forgive himself and his father. But Luke didn't actually know what Robert had said to help drive Carly away, so how could he forgive him? Besides, his father would never change. He wasn't greedy so much as he was determined to be in control, to make sure he got value for his dollar.

Luke knew that money wasn't as important as family. He was looking forward to spending time with Tom and Frances, Trent, Mia and little Max.

With a grin, he turned away from the window and picked up his suit jacket and briefcase. He wouldn't mind seeing Carly again, either. He remembered his promise to Lisa and Gemma, and he would do his best to keep that promise. Still, he wanted to see her. And he was heading to Reston tomorrow.

YAWNING AND WITH her favorite coffee cup in hand, Carly walked onto her porch and made herself comfortable on the front steps, turning slightly so that her back rested against the post that supported the railing. She tucked her robe around her legs and curled her toes into her slippers. The fall chill was only now making itself known and it would be a pleasant day for working in the garden. As her gaze drifted over her fields, she checked off the things she needed to do today and planned possible crops for next year. Lettuce always sold well, and even in rural Oklahoma, people liked variety. There were a few new varieties to consider, ones she hadn't grown before.

"Who on earth is that?" she whispered, sitting up suddenly. A man was stomping down the lane between her fields, seeming to list to one side as he did so.

It was several seconds before she could take in the camouflage outfit and focus on his face, which appeared to be smudged with green, brown and black paint. He wore one boot and was carrying the other.

Standing, she called out, "Jay? What are you doing?"

Right then, she heard the sound of small tires skidding on gravel and saw Sheena pedaling furiously up the drive.

The two of them met at the bottom of the porch steps and began talking at once.

"Are you all right?" Sheena demanded, leaning her bicycle against the porch railing.

"You were supposed to call me," Jay insisted, patting his numerous pockets, pulling out a cell phone and flipping it open. His face fell. "Oh. I guess I turned it off."

"Well, I knew something was wrong because I called you every two hours and you never answered."

"Sorry. I guess I fell asleep."

Sheena crossed her arms over her chest and looked at him with fear in her eyes. "I thought maybe you were dead or something or...or got eaten by a bear."

"A bear? I'd like to see one try."

"Wait, wait, wait." Carly held up her hands. "What's going on? Jay, why are you dressed like that? Have you been hunting?"

"Yeah, for turkey."

"What?"

Jay reached into the boot he was carrying and pulled out a piece of paper. "I thought I could catch whoever's been stealing your vegetables, but...I fell asleep. I was pretty tired and—"

"Jay," Sheena interrupted, pointing to the piece of paper. "Did the thief leave you a *note*?"

"Yeah, the little creeper. Took off my boot while I slept and stuck this inside."

Sheena grabbed the note he was waving in the air and read the childish block letters. "'Keep the snoring down. We're trying to sleep.'" With a snort of laughter, she said, "It's signed 'The animals.'"

Carly laughed, too, until she caught sight of Jay's red face. She cleared her throat and tried to look concerned. "That note was either written by an adult trying to write like a kid, or a kid with a sense of humor."

"Some sense of humor," Jay said scornfully. "At least now we know for sure it's not an animal 'cause they can't write lame-butt notes like this one." He sat to pull on his boot.

Sheena fought to control her laughter. "Did he untie your boot and take it off?"

"Yeah. I guess I oughta be glad he didn't tie my shoelaces together."

"I can't believe you slept through that."

"Can I help it if I'm a heavy sleeper?" Jay looked sheepish. "That's why I wanted you to call me, help me stay awake."

"It would have worked, too, if you hadn't turned your phone off in your sleep."

"Yeah. I'm gonna come up with a new plan."

Although she wanted nothing more than to laugh at Jay's annoyance, Carly had to be the adult voice of reason. "Jay, do your parents know where you spent the night?" The

Mortons were big believers in letting their kids develop their independence, but would they condone letting Jay sleep in her fields?

"Sure. I borrowed most of this gear from my dad. So, my new plan's gotta be one—"

"Where you don't fall asleep," Sheena teased. "And I won't be staying awake all night to help you." She smiled sheepishly. "Although, I may have dozed off for a few minutes, too."

He frowned at her. "Well, that wasn't any help, either."

"Which is why you need a new plan."

"Don't you have school today?" Carly asked.

"Yeah, I guess. That was the condition my mom and dad had—I had to get to school on time. But it's a late start today because of a teacher's meeting." He glanced at his cell phone to check the time. "All right, then I'll come up with a new plan after school." He looked at Sheena. "Can you help me get my gear from my camping spot?"

"Sleeping spot," she said, her eyes sparkling in delight. "Sure."

"Use the four-wheeler, Jay," Carly called after him. "It will be faster."

Before she left, Sheena turned the piece of paper over. "Look, Carly. There are dates and numbers written on it, starting last May. I wonder what they're for." With a shrug, she handed the paper to Carly and followed Jay.

Carly scanned the dates and numbers but couldn't decipher their meaning, either. She watched her helpers detour to the shed, chuckling to herself while she finished her coffee. Whoever the thief was, he'd met a worthy adversary in Jay Morton.

THE NEXT FEW DAYS passed with no more vegetables going missing, but Jay was convinced the thief would strike again and he planned to be ready for him. He arrived early on Sunday morning to help Carly reset the fence posts, but the thief was all he could talk about.

"I just can't figure out how the little creeper gets around without leaving footprints," he said as they drove to the boundary line above the apple orchard. "If I could see some prints, I could follow them, even set a trap—"

"No traps," Carly said firmly.

Jay didn't answer, but she knew this wasn't

the end of it. There was something about this intruder that really infuriated him. Probably because he'd been outsmarted.

When they reached the fence line, they saw the posts that had been leaning most precariously had been freed from their barbed wire, pulled up and set aside. Tools, including a posthole digger, were scattered on the ground.

"Whose are these?" Jay asked, indicating the equipment.

"Not mine. They're not even on my side of the fence line."

The sound of something being trundled over the crest of the hill drew them around to the sight of Luke Sanderson pushing a wheelbarrow filled with bags of cement.

"Morning," he called out. "Thought I'd be neighborly and reset your fence posts."

"Oh, that isn't necessary," Carly said hastily.

"It's a shared fence." Luke stopped the wheelbarrow on the slope and used rocks to brace the back supports until it sat evenly.

Carly watched him, momentarily distracted by the sure way he sorted the rocks and packed them into place. He looked very different today. A battle-scarred cowboy hat was settled on his head. He wore faded and holey jeans and a T-shirt sporting the logo of a construction company she'd never heard of.

When he caught her gaze on him, he gave a slight smile and said, "I've had plenty of wheelbarrows tip over on me or start rolling, even with only one wheel."

"It's nice of you to want to help, but it isn't necessary. I know how to reset fence posts. We couldn't get to it before, but we'll get it fixed today."

"But you don't need to do it alone. I'm here to help."

"Jay and I can do it," she insisted, needing to have the last word, even though Luke was ignoring her and Jay was staring at her curiously.

Luke began setting the bags of cement on the ground. Removing a bucket from the wheelbarrow, he walked to the stream and filled it with water.

"I'll reimburse you for the cement," Carly said. "My plan was to see how great the damage was before buying supplies."

"No need. We had some extra bags from

our project," Luke answered with a shrug. "I'm guessing the posts were loosened in the storms and then knocked down by the wind or maybe some wild animals."

"Did you see some? Or a person? Or some tracks?" Jay asked eagerly.

"Um, no. Didn't see anything." Luke raised an eyebrow.

"We've had an intruder who has taken some produce, being very careful to pick what he thinks we won't notice," Carly said.

"That's how we know it's not an animal," Jay said. "It's someone who's too lazy to get a job or grow his own food."

"Maybe. Or maybe he's just hungry," Luke pointed out.

"Then he could come to Carly's house and ask for food," Jay said, rolling his eyes. "Everyone knows she's a soft touch for a sad story. She's had me and Sheena taking food to Mrs. Salyer all summer."

"Jay," Carly admonished, stretching out his name so he'd get the hint that he was getting too worked up about the thief, but it didn't seem to be doing any good. Jay had started

walking around the downed fence posts, looking for tracks.

"Luke and I can work on the fence," she said to him as she pulled on thick work gloves and took a pair of wire cutters from her pocket. "There's no reason for three people to work on this. Why don't you pick about four dozen melons and get them ready to take to the supermarket tomorrow?" It was a new, late-ripening dwarf variety with intense flavor and she wanted to see how well it sold.

Jay tilted his head to one side then nodded. "Okay. But first, I'm going to take a look around and see if he's been back."

He headed off and Carly turned to look at Luke. She really didn't want to be alone with him, but there was no reason not to be. Besides, Jay was so distracted by their local thief, he might not be much help.

Also, that old saying about keeping your friends close and your enemies closer ran through her mind as she looked at the way the ground sloped downward from his property. Not that Luke was an enemy, but she certainly wanted to know what he was doing. Another saying sprang to mind—the one about catching more flies with honey than with vinegar.

Luke pulled out a pair of gloves and some wire cutters. "I'll start down here," he said, pointing toward the east end of the leaning fence. She nodded and climbed to the west side.

When they had all the strands of barbed wire free, they rolled them up one by one and set them aside.

Carly, who usually worked alone or with an employee she had to instruct, didn't know what to think of having a partner who seemed to know what he was doing. It made the job easier. She frowned, thinking that she'd never before associated the word *easy* with Luke Sanderson.

Once they finished with the wire, they began moving the posts, rocking them back and forth to pull them out of the ground. Then they used a short-handled sledgehammer to break off the remainder of the old concrete.

"That's why these fell over," Luke said. "Not enough concrete to hold the bases in place." He stopped and looked down the fence line. "I wonder who built this."

"Probably my dad," Carly said. "I doubt he'd ever built a fence before."

"Oh, well. It was pretty good for a first effort."

Luke pulled out a pocketknife, slit open the top of a bag of cement and poured it into the wheelbarrow, his muscles flexing as he lifted and lowered the bag to shake out all the thick powder.

Glancing up, he caught her watching him and couldn't seem to help grinning as he asked, "What are you looking at?"

She shook her head. "I honestly don't know. You don't look like you did three months ago, or even at the ice-cream social. Your hair is shaggy and you've got a week's growth of beard going on there." She made a vague gesture toward his jaw.

He tossed the emptied bag on the ground and said, "I'm not working in an office anymore."

"But you're not working as a carpenter. You're not in construction."

"Carly, what point are you trying to make?" His eyes took on a teasing light. "Are you saying you like what you see?"

She glanced away. "Oh, don't be ridiculous."

"You used to like my hair long, and you never minded when I didn't shave."

She gave him a too sweet smile. "Honestly? I hated it. It was prickly. It felt like I was kissing a toothbrush."

Luke burst out laughing. "Now why in the world would one look at my scruffy jaw make you think of kissing?"

She had no answer so she tossed her head, making her ponytail swing. "Are we going to finish these fence posts or not?"

He chuckled again. "Absolutely. Can you add water while I mix? If you can get your mind off kissing me, that is."

Casting him a dark look, Carly picked up the bucket of water and began pouring a steady stream while Luke used a shovel to mix the concrete to the right consistency. She found herself fascinated by the movement of the shovel, his biceps bunching and relaxing as he worked. When he looked up and grinned at what she knew must be her rapt expression, she glanced away, finding great interest in her apple trees, until he asked for her help.

Working together, they poured the concrete and set the posts in place. Luke even had a level, which he pulled from his pocket and set atop each post to make sure it was exactly right.

"We'll have to string the barbed wire tomorrow. Then the fence will be secure again," he said. "We can always put in a gate if you think we'll need one."

"Why would we need a gate?"

"In case you want to pay us a visit, maybe borrow a cup of sugar."

She shook her head. "I can't imagine any scenario where I would want to borrow something from Sanderson Enterprises."

The pleasure faded from his eyes. "You never know, Carly. We may turn out to be more useful than you think."

She doubted it, but maybe she was letting her worries about his project overrule her common sense.

"But, um, Carly, I was joking about paying us a visit. It would be better if you didn't come onto the job site."

"Rescinding your invitation already?" she asked, raising an eyebrow at him.

"Just thinking about your safety."

Or his own liability. All he'd done was raise her curiosity about what he would be doing.

"So… I need you to stay on your side of the fence…when it's finished."

Definitely thinking about liability, she concluded.

Reluctantly she nodded just as Jay returned. He'd picked and loaded the melons and found that at least a dozen of the cantaloupes were missing.

"So, Mr. Sanderson…" Jay said. "Even if he is hungry, nobody can eat twelve cantaloupe melons. Right, Carly? Nobody can eat that many by himself."

Carly suppressed a sigh. She wasn't going to hear the end of this until she let him pursue the thief. "You're right, Jay. I think it's time for you to give this your full attention. Catch the thief without harming him."

"You really want me to?" he asked eagerly.

"Absolutely."

Jay marched off triumphantly, his teenage brain already full of plans.

"And no traps," she called after him. "Use your ingenuity."

"Not sure I've got it. I think I left it in my camo pants."

"Jay…" she called out again, but he answered with a laugh.

"You're seriously going to let him spend time on this?" Luke asked.

"Why not? I'm not going to get any more work out of him until he solves this mystery. Besides, he's a sixteen-year-old kid taking the initiative on something that will benefit people other than himself. That is behavior that needs to be encouraged."

LUKE WATCHED JAY for another second. He was a man on a mission, determined to catch the thief and make him pay.

"You're probably right," he said slowly. "It might be really good for him to be responsible for the outcome. Let's hope it's a good one."

"I'll keep an eye on him, make sure he's got a reasonable plan."

Luke nodded thoughtfully. As they cleaned up their tools and headed to their opposite sides of the fence, he tried to compare the confident, self-assured woman next door to the skittish, unsure one he'd known a dozen years ago. He couldn't make a successful comparison—they were like two different people.

CARLY FINISHED DINNER and went out to the porch to sit for a minute. Ordinarily she would be working on one of her refurbishing projects, but since most of her stock was already in Upcycle, she was at loose ends—a rarity for her.

She could already see that once her shop took off, as Lisa was so sure it would, the biggest challenge was going to be keeping up her stock. In that case, Lisa would have to go along on scavenging trips, her least favorite thing. Maybe Gemma would come, too, if she was willing to take an afternoon away from her new husband or the Sunshine Birthing Center.

Carly gave a nostalgic sigh. She, Lisa and Gemma had been best friends all their lives, maintaining their relationship through detours to college, Carly's own short marriage and Gemma's nursing career in Tulsa. Now things were changing again and, for the most part, she liked what was happening, but she hoped that closeness didn't change.

In the growing dusk, she could see that her fields and greenhouses were bedded down for the night, with more crops to pick tomorrow. The pumpkins were getting ripe and would soon be ready for visits from the local elementary schools where kindergarteners and first-graders would pick a pumpkin to take home. She never made much money on her pumpkin patch, but it was a service to the community. And, besides, it was impossible to put a price on the joy in a kid's face when he picked out the pumpkin he loved. The teachers often sent photos of the jack-o'-lanterns the children created. Carly tacked them up on the bulletin board in her kitchen.

A flash of light caught her attention and she looked over toward the Withers place. Luke's place, she corrected herself. She knew they were only in the initial phases of the process but she was wildly curious to see even a small part of it. After all, it was almost certain to affect her life and her livelihood, and this might be her only chance to walk over the hill to see it. After this, she would have to drive around to the other side of the property to the new access road.

She had heard the deep rumble of diesel engines pulling trailers of equipment onto the site and she wanted to know how it was going to be used.

Luke didn't seem to grasp how vital her property was to her. She wanted to trust him, but how could she when he wouldn't tell her what she needed to know?

It wouldn't hurt to take a little peek, she decided, simply a quick in and out.

Standing, she grabbed the adjustable-beam flashlight she kept by the back door, took an aimless stroll around her property to make sure no one was watching, then headed up the lane to where she and Luke had reset fence posts that day. She'd decided not to take the four-wheeler. Too noisy.

The night was cool but cloudless, so it was easy to see the path she needed to take. She was glad for the jacket she'd pulled on but wondered if she should have borrowed some camouflage makeup from Jay.

Treading carefully, she made her way past the bare fence posts and moved into the shadows. The glow of lights drew her forward, just beyond the crest of the hill. Although she felt utterly foolish, Carly crouched and then dropped down to do the belly crawl so she could get as close as possible without being seen.

Loose shale and gravel bit into her hands and rolled away beneath her palms. She slowed her movements as she tried to minimize the noise.

Pulling herself along, she was delighted to find she had an excellent view of the entire work area—although now that she'd gone to all this trouble, there wasn't much to see. The motor home Jay had seen was parked to one side, along with Luke's truck, and beside it was a corrugated tin shed with the mobile office, lengths of pipe and some other equipment covered by blue plastic tarps.

Propping her chin on her stacked fists, she studied the area and tried to determine what the extraction process would involve. There wasn't anything unusual to give her a hint, except the pipe. It would be driven deep into the ground. Chemicals would be added, and pressure, too, using some kind of power source. That's how fracking worked.

The shed probably held equipment, the purpose of the mobile office was self-evident, and the motor home was likely where Luke would be living.

"But who was the woman?" she whispered, recalling that Jay had seen a lady driving the motor home. Maybe she had been the one delivering it. Hadn't he mentioned a VW Bug, as well? Maybe it was parked on the other side of the motor home.

"Did you find what you're looking for?"

CHAPTER EIGHT

WITH A SQUEAK of surprise, Carly flipped onto her back and stared up at him.

"Luke, you startled me."

"Well, imagine my surprise when I went to dampen the concrete around the fence posts and saw you sneak past then fall down and crawl. Were you trying to get a drop on the enemy?"

Sitting up, she tried for some dignity. "We're not at war. I was just curious. I wanted to see what you're doing over here since you can't seem to share any information with me, even though it affects my land, as well." She started to get to her feet and when he reached down a hand to help her up, she refused it, but the shale and gravel shifted beneath her boots.

"Oh!" She began sliding backward down the slope until her feet went out from beneath her and she toppled onto her back.

Luke made a grab for her but missed, falling as he overcorrected his balance and followed her down on his stomach.

"Umph," she grunted as she slid to a stop at the bottom of the slope. She stared up at the night sky and tried to get her breath back.

Luke recovered more quickly than she did, crawling over to her as he said, "Carly, are you okay? Are you hurt?"

"I…doh…hon't think so." Her breath came in wheezes as Luke helped her up. "How about you?"

"Yeah, I'm okay." He dusted himself off. "I think I ripped my jeans."

"How can you tell?" she asked, glancing at the worn denim of his pants as she steadied herself.

He only gave her a steady look she could barely see in the dim light and said, "Now, do you understand why I said for you to stay away?"

Carly gingerly moved her arms and twisted to feel movement in her back, then reached behind her to scoop gravel from her back pockets. "Yeah, I understand, but I'm here now, so why don't you show me around?" She took out her flashlight to brighten the path.

"I'm not going to give you the grand tour but—"

"Can you at least tell me where the drill itself will be?" she asked, determined that defying his request and sliding down a hill on her back should gain her at least one piece of information tonight.

"Sure." He pointed toward a rise that was barely on his side of the fence line.

"Of course," she murmured in dismay. "So I can see the lovely thing from anywhere on my property."

He didn't respond to her comment, but instead asked, "Would you like to meet Shelby?"

"The scientist who's developing this mysterious process? Sure."

"This way. Watch your step," he advised. "There's still a slope here. It can be slippery going down."

"I'm recently familiar with the properties of shale, thank you," she answered in a sarcastic tone, but she turned and followed him down the hillside and into the clearing.

"Are you two sharing the motor home?" Carly asked, dusting herself off again, then removing her denim jacket and giving it a good shake. It didn't seem to be too much the worse for wear.

Luke smiled as he walked up the steps and knocked on the door. "I didn't think you'd be that interested in my living arrangements."

"I'm not."

"I'm staying with Tom and Frances. This is Shelby's home."

When the door started to open, Luke stepped aside to reveal a woman standing in the doorway.

"Oh, hi, Luke. I thought you'd left. Come on in." She stepped back but when she saw Carly, she gave Luke a swift look and said, "Oh, hello."

"Dr. Shelby Wayne, this is Carly Joslin. She owns Joslin Gardens, right next door."

"Oh, yes, I've seen the signs and your produce stand. In fact, I stopped to buy some squash and tomatoes. Delicious. Um, come in. Sit down."

Once inside the cozy living quarters, Carly could see that Shelby Wayne was a very pretty woman who appeared to be in her fifties. She had dark eyes and curly brown hair, peppered with gray, which was cut in a short, convenient style. She moved with graceful gestures and her hands were more beautiful and artistic than Carly would have expected a scientist's to be.

Dr. Wayne offered them something to drink, and when they both refused, an awkward silence followed.

Carly stumbled into speech. "This is a nice place," she said, looking around at the living room and the minuscule kitchen. "I've always been amazed at how the builders can fit everything in."

"Um, yes." Shelby gave her a nervous glance and pressed her palms together.

Luke seemed to pick up on this, so he said, "Carly is very curious about what we're doing here."

"Well, that's understandable," Shelby said cautiously. "Wouldn't you be? Some aspects of gas extraction don't have the best reputation."

Carly relaxed, glad that Shelby seemed to understand.

"However," Shelby went on, "I'm afraid I can't tell you anything except that we'll do our best to limit the impact we have on the local environment."

Not exactly a guarantee, Carly thought. "But your process will involve chemicals, possibly injected into the ground, right?"

Shelby bit her lip. "I'm sorry. I can't say. It's a process I've been working on for a while, but at this point, it's secret. You see, I developed another process a couple of years ago, but it was…stolen, so I don't share any of my procedures or notes."

"The agreement I have with Shelby is that I'll provide the funds, help when I'm needed, but generally stay out from underfoot."

Carly sighed. Shelby looked as though she really wanted Carly to let this go, and Luke was watching her warily.

While she could understand Shelby's reluctance, she didn't like not knowing what was going on. She had spent twelve years making sure she was in control of her life, gardens, finances—everything she *could* control. She was able to handle the unexpected things that happened, even make them work for her sometimes—the summer's overwhelming rain had meant she didn't have to water her gardens, making it possible to replace part of the sprinkler system that had seen so many years of use. This was different, though. She had no control over any part of it—except for her reaction to the situation.

Finally she smiled. "I appreciate your concerns, but if anything happens that I need to know about, any mishap that might affect my gardens, you'll let me know, right?"

Shelby nodded with relief. "Of course."

"I'll drive you home, Carly."

She said good-night to Shelby and stepped outside. When Luke joined her, she said, "I can find my own way home, Luke."

She started toward the house, and he stepped in front of her. "Has all of this been worth it? Did you learn anything?"

"You know I didn't, Luke. It was an exercise in futility."

He gave her a cold glare. "Then stay out of it."

"It's my livelihood, Luke! People are depending on me."

They were at an impasse, feet stubbornly planted on each side of a dividing line.

She stepped around him to stalk away, but

he said, "At least let me walk you home. It's getting late and it's the gentlemanly thing to do. Omi would say my manners could use some brushing up."

"She would be right."

Because they had to watch where they were walking, they didn't talk much until they reached Carly's porch.

"I forgot to leave the porch light on," Carly said, placing her hand on the familiar railing and mounting the steps.

"You probably didn't need it for your nighttime reconnaissance mission," Luke responded in a dry tone.

"Not when I've got my trusty flashlight," she answered, patting her pocket. When she turned around to say good-night, he was taking a seat on the top step.

"Okay if I sit down?" he asked.

"I thought it was past your bedtime." She sat at the other end of the wide step and turned toward him, resting her back against the post.

"Yeah, but I wanted to tell you I didn't make specific plans for any of this to happen. Not here and not now. Not right next to you.

The corporation owns other properties, but this one is the best bet for Shelby's process."

"Oh, why is that?"

"It's rural, not too many neighbors. A stranger would be noticed if they were trying to spy on her process."

Carly smiled. "Unless they were as successful at hiding their presence as our produce thief."

"Yeah, I guess."

"So, her process is that valuable, hmm?"

"I think it can be. All she needs is time to develop it."

"But she's only got six months, right?"

"Thanks to my dad's deadline, that's right."

"I'm still confused about how you even got into the natural gas extraction business."

"By accident," he answered on a sigh.

"Wendolin told me that after we…broke up, you left Dallas, worked on building projects in South America."

"That's true, and I wasn't management, either. I was a carpenter."

She smiled into the darkness. "That was always your favorite type of job. How did your father feel about that?"

"Oh, he wasn't happy, but it suited me for a long time. Then I ended up on an oil field and got interested in the energy business at about the same time Sanderson Enterprises invested a boatload of cash in oil. It seemed to me that there could be more efficient ways of producing energy, more sustainable ways. Nobody wanted to hear that from a carpenter, though, so I came home, went back to university, took some chemistry and environmental science classes along with engineering, and tried to make a few changes in the way my dad does business."

"How has that worked out for you?"

"You've met my dad. What do you think?"

Robert Sanderson wasn't someone she wanted to spend her mental energy on, especially not this late at night, but she knew the more information she had, the better.

"I think he gave you an ultimatum and not much time to finish what you had to do."

"Yes. The big changes in the oil industry have had an enormous impact on him and his company. He's not seeing the kinds of profits he's seen in the past. No one is, and while some of the smaller producers are sticking with petroleum, he wants to cut his losses. Most of his management people agree with him."

"So why *this* project?" she asked, pointing toward the rise of land that would soon be graced with a drilling rig. "Why Shelby's process?"

"She was a friend of my mom's. Shelby told me about her stolen process and her passion for developing an extraction method that was more environmentally friendly than some of the current ones."

Carly glanced out at her darkened fields, wondering how friendly the process would be to her environment, but her thoughts circled back to Robert.

Luke's father wasn't opposed to new ideas, as long as he was in complete control, and as long as it made a significant profit. That was what every business owner wanted, her included. Carly frowned at the thought that she was anything like Robert.

"Well, I guess I've overstayed my welcome," Luke said, getting to his feet. "So I'll say goodnight."

At that moment the yard lights blazed on,

the sprinklers came to life and someone released a surprised yelp.

"What in the world?" Carly jumped up and tried to see what was happening.

"There he is! I see him!" a voice yelled from somewhere near the shed. "Come on."

As Carly and Luke watched, two figures detached themselves from the shadowy doorway of the shed and dashed toward the fields. She immediately recognized Jay but couldn't see who the other person was, though she didn't think it was Sheena.

Carly couldn't see who they were chasing but, alarmed at the purposeful way the two were running, she took off after them with Luke close behind.

They had only run a few yards when the lights went out. Carly stopped suddenly, fumbling for her flashlight, and Luke ran into her.

"Oof," she grunted, stumbling forward. "Watch where you're going."

Luke grabbed her around the waist before she went down. "It's kind of hard in the dark," he shot back, steadying her on her feet before letting her go.

As soon as Carly got her flashlight out and

switched it on, the yard lights came on again and the sprinklers went off. Jay and the other person took off again, so she and Luke rejoined the chase.

As they dashed up the lane between the fields, she could see Jay stretch out midair in a full-on tackle. He wrapped his arms around the other runner's legs, and the two of them landed with a crash that brought down two poles of green beans and a tomato cage.

Carly and Luke ran up at the same time as Jay's companion.

"Owen Forester?" Carly said, recognizing the high schooler who was supposed to be at home updating her Upcycle website. "What are you doing here?"

"He's helping me," Jay said, sitting up triumphantly and untangling himself from a slim pole and a thick vine. Leaning over, he grabbed a flailing arm and pulled someone to their feet.

"I got you, you little creep," he said, then looked up with a huge grin. "Carly, here's our thief."

Carly dimmed her flashlight and turned the beam on the person Jay held prisoner. It was a skinny, mop-haired kid with a bean vine over one shoulder and a beefsteak tomato smashed against the side of his head. His thin T-shirt was wet from where the sprinkler had hit him full in the chest. Angry eyes flashed at her as his mouth hardened into a stiff line.

"Why, he's just a boy," she said. "Who are you?"

When he didn't answer, she looked from Jay to Owen. "Do you guys know who this is?"

"Never seen him before," Owen answered.

Jay shook his head, too. When the boy's shoulders slumped, Jay seemed to take pity on him and released his tight hold.

Seeing his chance, the boy started to take off, but Luke hooked an arm around his waist and said, "Hold on, son. Nobody's going to hurt you."

The boy jerked out of his grasp and stood with his head down. When Carly saw his shoulders shake, followed by a wipe of his eyes with the back of his hand, her heart clenched with sympathy.

"Wait," Luke said after a second. He took off his denim jacket and placed it around the boy's shoulders. "I know you. Dustin, right? I gave you and your bike and your boxes a ride into town one time, remember? I'm Luke Sanderson."

Dustin nodded but still didn't answer.

"What's your last name? Where do you live?" Luke continued. "I asked my aunt to check on you, but she couldn't find out anything."

"And why are you stealing from Carly?" Jay asked, obviously reluctant to let go of what he considered to be the real issue here. "Talk or we're calling the sheriff."

"Jay," Carly said in her warning tone.

"Well, he's been stealing." Jay picked up a gunny sack. Reaching inside, he pulled out a handful of green beans. "See?"

"Maybe he's hungry," Luke pointed out, repeating what he'd said earlier.

Jay snorted in disbelief, but Carly laid a gentle hand on Dustin's shoulder and felt too prominent bones beneath her palm. He was almost certainly hungry. "Tell us your name. We promise we won't be calling the sheriff. We want to help you."

He shook his shoulder and Carly took the hint, lifting her hand away from him.

"It's Salyer." Dustin spoke so low, they could barely hear him.

"Salyer. You're Era's grandson," Carly said, bending close. She resisted the urge to push back his hair and pluck the squashed tomato out of it. He didn't seem to appreciate being touched. "I haven't seen you since you were a baby. I didn't even know you were visiting her."

"Nobody does." The tone of his voice was flat and dull. Hopeless.

"How long have you been with her? I haven't seen you around."

"Awhile," he muttered.

"I'm Carly Joslin. This is my property. I'm a friend of Mrs. Salyer's. I've known her all of my life and I know there's no way she would condone you coming over here and taking things. Does she know where you are?"

"No. She's asleep. She sleeps a lot."

A wave of shame swept over Carly at the way she'd neglected her neighbor all summer. "Is she sick?"

He nodded. "I think so. I been taking her vegetables and apples, but she's no better."

"We need to go see about her."

"I'll come with you," Luke said immediately. He reached for his cell phone. "And I'll call 9-1-1."

"No. I'll call Gemma and Nathan."

When he gave Carly a puzzled look, she said, "Gemma's a nurse, remember? And her husband is the doctor who's reopening the hospital, though that won't be for a week or two. Whatever is wrong with Era, it's probably better for them to start treatment now and then call the paramedics."

"Oh, right."

Carly quickly called Gemma, waking both her and her husband, but they said they would be at Era's house as fast as possible.

As the group started walking back toward her house, Carly saw Jay look over at Owen and grin.

"You run pretty good for a geek," he said.

"For a jock, your computer skills aren't too bad," Owen responded. "But we need to find out why the lights went off and came back on. That wasn't supposed to be in the setup."

"In the trap, you mean."

The two boys laughed, obviously proud of themselves for having caught Dustin.

Carly wasn't quite as thrilled about it as they were. Although she admitted, to her shame, that she had told him to catch the thief. But she hadn't suspected the miscreant was an underfed kid.

"What did you guys do?" she asked.

"Owen helped me set up a motion detector on the lights and the sprinklers. I knew we could catch this guy if he got hit by the lights and the sprinklers at the same time."

"Jay, he's a kid," Luke put in before Carly could speak.

"Well, yeah, but I didn't know that, did I?" Jay's voice had turned sullen.

"And I told you no traps," Carly said. Her pride in Jay's initiative was quickly turning sour.

"He didn't get hurt!"

"Where did you get a motion detector?" Carly asked.

"I took it off my dad's machine shop," Owen volunteered. "It switches on the lights when something moves. My mom hates it 'cause the lights flash whenever a stray cat walks by. She won't care if it's gone."

"But your dad might. He's got it on his shop for a reason. You undo and unwire everything you rigged up and get the motion detector back where it belongs," Luke said. "Do your parents know where you are?"

"Sure." Owen looked insulted. "I told them I was helping Jay with a project."

"Awesome project," Jay said, obviously still buzzed about its success.

Carly knew it was going to take a lot more talking for Jay to understand the harm that might have come from his scheme. She decided to tackle it later.

"After you replace the motion detector, both of you go home and go to bed. As far as I know, you've still got school tomorrow," she said.

"Sheesh," Jay grumbled. "You'd think some people would show a little appreciation around here."

The two teenagers hurried away, talking excitedly.

While Luke and Dustin climbed into her truck, Carly ran inside to get the keys. When she slid in behind the wheel, she and Luke looked at each other over the head of the wet, bedraggled boy between them. Luke gave her an encouraging smile and a shrug.

Within a few minutes they were pulling up in front of Era's house, which was completely dark.

"Dustin, is the house locked?"

"Yeah. I don't want nobody going in and bothering my grandma. I use the window."

When neither adult moved right away, he sighed. "I ain't gonna run away. You'd just call the sheriff to come find me. And he'd put me in jail. Maybe put Grandma in jail."

"No one's going to jail," Luke assured him as he stepped out of the truck. "Go on in and open the front door for us."

Dustin hurried around the side of the house and, within a couple of minutes, lights flicked on and the front door opened.

Inside, Carly was shocked at the messy state of the house. She had been in here many times and had never seen it like this.

"Where is your grandmother?" Luke asked.

"Her room is this way," Carly answered,

heading down the hallway and flicking on lights as she went.

In Era's room, she switched on the bedside lamp, which caused the older lady to groan. She turned her face away, but Carly bent over her and gently took her hand, which was hot to the touch. Alarmed, she felt Era's face.

"She's burning up with fever," she said over her shoulder. "I was wrong, Luke. Better call the paramedics right away. I know that's what Nathan would recommend."

With a nod, he hurried from the room.

Carly rushed to the bathroom, where she dampened a washcloth and brought it back to bathe Era's face. Seeing a water glass with a straw on the nightstand, she placed the straw between Era's lips and tried to get her to drink. The older lady took a couple of sips, but struggled to open her eyes as she murmured, "Don't go outside. Don't let them see you."

Carly thought she might be delirious. Talking softly, she assured her friend that everything would be okay, but she received no response. Pulling up a chair, she held Era's hand.

"I tried to take care of her," Dustin said from where he stood in the corner of the room.

Startled, Carly looked around. In her concern for Era, she'd forgotten about him. She tried to give him a reassuring smile.

"I'm sure you did. How long has she been like this?"

"Just today. She cut her arm a couple of days ago, but yesterday, she could get up and go to the bathroom and stuff."

"Cut her arm?" Carly lifted Era's right arm, and then her left, where she saw a long red cut on the inside of her upper arm.

"I put a bandage on it, but it fell off."

"Do you know how she cut it?"

Dustin looked at her suspiciously for a few seconds, as if trying to figure out if she was accusing him of something. Finally he said, "She went down to the road to get the mail. When she was coming back, she got dizzy or something and fell. I think she tried to grab the gate, but something sharp cut her. I helped her get in the house and then I put a bandage on the cut."

"When you saw how sick she was, why didn't you call for help? Call 9-1-1?"

"She told me not to, said they'd put her in jail."

"*Who* did she think would put her in jail?"

Dustin hitched up one shoulder in a shrug. "The sheriff, I guess."

Which explained his fear of the sheriff, Carly thought, but not why Era had feared arrest.

"Don't worry," she said, giving him an encouraging smile. "No one is going to call the sheriff. We just want to make sure your grandma is okay."

The boy's dark eyes searched her face, as if he wanted to believe her, but before he responded they heard voices in the living room and then Gemma and Nathan hurried into the room.

Relieved that the professionals had arrived, Carly told them what she knew, showed them the inside of Era's arm and then ushered Dustin from the room. "Come on, Dustin," she said. "They'll take care of her. We'll wait out here."

In the living room, he sat in an armchair and gazed anxiously toward the hallway, waiting for news. Carly, full of nervous energy, began straightening the room and carrying dirty dishes to the kitchen, where she found Luke filling the sink with soapy water and rolling up his sleeves.

When she gave a small, surprised laugh, he glanced around. "I'm not good at waiting. Thought maybe I could help."

"I'm sure Era would appreciate it."

She told him about Era's cut and he said, "There's no food in the place except for a dozen melons in the refrigerator. So, Jay was right."

"Yes." She looked back toward the living room, where Dustin appeared to have fallen asleep. "What was he going to do with a dozen melons?"

"No idea, but that may have been all he and his grandmother had to eat." He nodded toward the back door. "And there must be a hundred empty canning jars out there."

Guiltily, she nodded and turned away as she tried to recall the last time she had brought food over, or had one of her employees drop some off. It had been a couple of weeks. But why hadn't Era called her? Asked for help?

She stepped out the back door and looked

at the rows of clean, empty canning jars and felt even guiltier. Era had canned her fruits and vegetables for years. Since she hadn't raised a garden this year, she and Dustin had eaten up her stock. Their diet had been supplemented by what Dustin had taken from Joslin Gardens.

Something strange was going on here, and she had no idea what it was. She thought back to the early summer day when Sheena had told her there was something wrong with Era, but Era hadn't seemed to want help, or company. Was that when all of this, whatever it was, had started?

Era was only seventy, hardly in her dotage, but was it possible she had early-onset dementia?

Her troubled thoughts were interrupted by Gemma, who came in to say, "Era's seriously ill. That cut has turned septic."

Luke dried his hands on a kitchen towel, which he tossed over his shoulder as he came to stand beside Carly. "And that means blood poisoning, right?"

Gemma's astounded gaze went from him to the sink full of soapy water and back.

"Yes. I've called the paramedics again. They're still ten minutes out, and this place might be hard to find in the dark."

Luke held out his hand. "Carly, have you still got your flashlight? I'll go out onto the highway and flag them down."

She handed it over and he hurried outside.

Gemma stared after him. "Well, of all the people I ever expected to see standing in Era Salyer's kitchen washing dishes, Luke Sanderson would have been the last one on the list. I'm dying to know what's going on, but right now we have a patient. Don't think I won't bring this up again."

"I know you will," Carly said with a smile.

Gemma hurried out, muttering, "Five days. Only five more days and we'll have the hospital open."

Carly checked on Dustin, who was sound asleep. Now that he was still, and she could get a good look at him, she saw that he looked like his father—Era's son, Joseph—who had died a few years ago in an oil field accident. But where was the boy's mother? And how old was Dustin now? She tried to think back, to recall when Dustin had been born, when Era had proudly showed her pictures of him.

The memory came back with a pang. It had been a few months after she'd miscarried her own son, after she and Luke had broken up.

Carly swallowed the lump in her throat as she recalled Era's excitement. She had chattered on and on about the baby, blissfully unaware of Carly's pain. After all these years, the memory still hurt even though she knew Era had meant no harm.

Glancing around the living room, Carly saw the same photograph of a dark-eyed, chubby baby boy.

He was twelve. Dustin was the same age as Carly's own son would have been. She picked up one of Era's many crocheted throws and spread it over him, noting again how skinny and generally unkempt he was. He and his grandmother had struggled to take care of themselves, but she didn't understand why they had thought it was necessary to go it alone.

CHAPTER NINE

LUKE FINISHED THE phone calls he'd needed to make and stood on Carly's porch, sipping coffee and watching the sun stretch its early morning rays over the rows of vegetables. They'd had a heck of a night. It had been close to one o'clock in the morning when Mrs. Salyer had been transported by ambulance to the hospital in Toncaville, accompanied by Gemma and Nathan. He and Carly had brought the still-sleeping Dustin to Carly's house.

The ride home had been quite a revelation. He'd driven Carly's truck while she had cradled the boy close in spite of the dirt all over him and the tomato smashed into his shaggy hair. The tender look on her face for this ragged boy had nearly stopped his heart. He hoped he could be as gentle and forgiving of a thief as she was. When they reached her house, he'd carried Dustin inside where she had tucked him into bed in her guest room before stumbling off to bed herself.

She had told Luke good-night, obviously expecting him to leave, but he was concerned about how Dustin was going to react when he woke up in a strange place. From what he'd seen, the boy was feisty and unpredictable. Carly would probably need help with him. Besides, Luke admitted to himself, he was curious about the boy who had been in the area with his grandmother for months, raiding Carly's gardens, too terrified to ask for help. Hoping to get answers this morning, Luke had made himself comfortable on Carly's sofa and had actually slept for a few hours.

"Are you back already?" Carly asked from the doorway.

He turned around to see her watching him with sleepy eyes as she pushed her tangled hair out of her face. Oh, yeah, he remembered that about her. She had usually awakened looking as if she'd been wrestling bears all night.

"I slept on your couch. Figured I'd done enough stumbling around in the dark for one night." He held up the cup. "I made coffee."

"Nectar of the gods," she murmured, letting the door close behind her as she started for the kitchen.

He chuckled to himself and sat on the steps. She was back twenty minutes later, her hair brushed into its usual smooth ponytail, dressed in jeans and a long-sleeved, blue T-shirt with the Joslin Gardens logo on the front and back. She was carrying a cup of coffee and two cinnamon rolls. She handed him one, then joined him on the steps.

"Thanks," he said, taking a big bite. He hadn't realized how hungry he was. "You know, you should have a couple of lounge chairs out here."

Carly snickered. "When would I have time to lounge around on the porch?"

"Maybe you work too hard."

"Maybe I do." She looked around. "I used to have Adirondack chairs. My mom and dad and I would sit out here and talk about what we needed to do around the gardens, until my dad got sick, that is, and they moved to Tulsa."

She took another bite of her cinnamon roll and gave it an appreciative look. "These rolls remind me of that time, too. My mom shared her cinnamon roll recipe with Stephanie Hardcastle. When Stephanie started her bakery in town, she began making these and calls them Angie's Buns." Carly chuckled. "I don't think my mom is crazy about that name."

This was the first she had spoken about that time and he wouldn't mind if she continued. Keeping his voice carefully neutral, he asked, "What did you do with the chairs?"

"Painted them bright blue and sold them to the Mortons. They're still in their backyard. That was my first up-cycling project. I discovered I liked it and I'm good at it."

"And look how far you've come. Now you have your own shop."

"Yes." She gazed out at her fields. "And my gardens—at least for now."

Unwilling to get into the fracking conversation again, he said, "I called the hospital. They would only say that Mrs. Salyer is resting comfortably."

"They told me the same thing, so I called Gemma, who said she'll be in the hospital for several days on intravenous antibiotics, then probably in the rehabilitation center next door to the hospital for physical therapy."

"I'm glad she's getting good care." Luke took a sip of coffee. "The question is what are we going to do about Dustin?"

THEY WERE TALKING about him. Dustin had been awake for a while, looking around this room with its pink-painted walls, trying to figure out where he was. He'd made a surreptitious trip to the bathroom and when he'd returned, he'd opened the window, in case he needed to climb out of it and run. He'd fallen back asleep, awakened again, and now he realized the window overlooked the front porch, where he could hear those two grown-ups from last night talking about him.

That had happened before. It always meant trouble. It meant his mom's latest boyfriend was sick of him, wanted him gone. Well, the last time, he'd saved them the trouble of shipping him off to a relative he didn't even know, or putting him in foster care. He'd taken off and found his grandmother.

But now she was going to die and he didn't know what he was going to do. He'd heard them talking last night, using words like *blood poisoning*. He didn't know exactly what that was, but he knew what poison was. His grandma was poisoned, and it was probably his fault. He'd tried to take care of her, get her food, but he'd failed. An ambulance had come and they'd taken her away. Now he could hear them saying she was getting good care, but he was still afraid she might die.

He turned on his side and gripped his empty stomach as he fought the tears welling in his eyes. He'd have to run again. But where would he go this time?

"THE FIRST THING we need to do is feed him," Carly said. "And then take him to see Era."

They heard something hit the floor in the guest room. Carly set down her cup and walked cautiously across the creaky wooden porch to peek in the window. At the same time, Luke crossed the porch and eased open the door, disappearing inside.

Carly could see Dustin, with his shoes clutched to his chest, reaching for the door-knob. When he looked over his shoulder, their eyes met and he froze.

"Good morning," she called through the open window. "Don't you want some breakfast? Do you like pancakes? Bacon? Eggs? I can fix whatever you'd like."

He hesitated, but he still reached for the doorknob. When he swung the door open, Luke was standing there.

"Hey, buddy," Luke greeted him. "Aren't you hungry?"

Dustin's head tipped forward for a second but then he straightened. "Maybe," he said. "But I gotta go see about Grandma."

"She's in the hospital."

Seeing that Dustin wasn't going to flee—at least not through the window—Carly hurried into the house and joined Luke in the hallway.

"She's getting good care," Luke continued. "But she'll be in the hospital for a few days."

"I'll take you to visit her in a little while so you can see for yourself," Carly said, trying for a firm, nonthreatening tone. "In the meantime, I'll fix you something to eat, and you can take a shower." She smiled. "You might want to wash the smashed tomato out of your hair."

Dustin reached up, felt his matted and dirty

hair, and said, "Yeah, okay, but I don't have clean clothes to put on."

"You can borrow some of mine," she said brightly, startling a disbelieving snort of laughter out of him. "Well, maybe not. While you shower and I cook, maybe Luke can go over to your grandmother's house and get you some clothes."

"I don't have no clean clothes there, either. We ran out of soap."

"Then Luke will gather up your dirty things and bring them over here. We'll wash and dry what you need."

The two males looked at her, then at each other.

"She's kind of bossy," Dustin said.

"So it seems," Luke answered, holding out his hand to Carly. "I'll need to use your truck. Mine's still over at the job site."

She snagged her keys from the hook beside the back door and he left to do her bidding. Searching through the guest room closet, she found an old bathrobe of her dad's and got Dustin headed into the bathroom with everything he needed, including a brand-new toothbrush.

Once the door was shut behind him, she quickly got breakfast started, then began making a list of everything she needed to do that day. Running two businesses and trying to make up for neglecting her neighbor would make this a frantically busy day.

Luke returned with an armload of clothing, but when she tried to take it from him, he pulled it away. "I know how to do laundry, Carly. Just point me to the washer."

She directed him to the laundry facilities on the back porch and returned to the kitchen. Some things had changed in twelve years. When they'd been married, he had never done his own laundry, hadn't even known how.

She was draining bacon on paper towels and had finished the first stack of pancakes when Dustin sidled uncertainly into the room, holding up the hem of her dad's old robe so he wouldn't trip on it and clutching his dirty clothes to his chest. His hair was slicked back, emphasizing the prominence of his cheekbones and the thinness of his face. A small bruise darkened the skin above his eye, probably a result of Jay's flying tackle.

Even though guilt kicked at her, she gave

him a bright smile as she took the clothes from him and carried them to Luke, then put several pancakes and some slices of bacon on a plate and handed it to him. "Have a seat and dig in, Dustin."

She didn't have to ask him twice. He sat quickly and poured a lake of syrup over his breakfast. He began devouring it and was half-finished by the time she set a glass of milk in front of him.

Luke walked in and stopped in surprise. "Hey, slow down, buddy, or you'll make yourself sick."

Dustin gave him a look that questioned his sanity, but he did start taking an occasional breath between bites.

Carly and Luke ate, too, and the three of them were finishing up when they heard the crunch of gravel beneath tires. She set her plate in the sink and walked out to see a sheriff's car stopping by her front steps, and Deputy Wayne Fedder Jr.—known as Junior to everyone—stepping out.

She smiled at the sight of him. Dangerously overweight until his girlfriend had said she wouldn't marry him until he got healthy, he'd lost a considerable number of pounds and now moved like the young man he was instead of an ancient one.

She held the door open for him. "Hey, Junior," she said. "What brings you out this morning?"

He gave her a puzzled look as he stepped inside. He was carrying a small laptop case. "Sheriff Held sent me, said—"

"You said you wouldn't call the sheriff." Dustin spoke furiously from the doorway. "You said no one would call the sheriff and try to arrest my grandma...or...or me."

Carly held out her hands, palms up. "I didn't, Dustin. I promise."

"I did," Luke said, standing behind the boy but looking at Carly. "I didn't know Carly had promised that, but, Dustin, when a kid's been left by himself, even for a while, the authorities need to know."

"That's why you took my clothes," Dustin said, "so I couldn't run away." Jerking the oversize robe above his ankles, he stomped down the hallway and slammed the door to the guest room.

Luke started after him, but Carly said, "Better give him a while to cool down."

Junior gave them an apologetic look as he said, "Carly, can we sit down and have a cup of coffee? I think we might be having a long talk."

"Oh, of course."

In the kitchen, she poured fresh coffee for all three of them, then she and Luke watched as Junior took a notebook computer out of its case and set it up on the table.

"The thing is," he said. "Dustin Salyer is a runaway." He tapped the keys and pulled up a photo, which he turned to show them. It was Dustin, all right. A school photo of him with a better haircut, a solemn expression and a hint of defiance in his eyes. "He took off from his mother's place in Waco, Texas, in May. She turned in a report, said maybe he'd come up here to Era's. I talked to Era then, but she said he wasn't there. We checked back a couple of times, but she said he'd never turned up." He shook his head. "I've known Mrs. Salyer my whole life. She and my mom used to play Bunco together. I can't believe she lied to my face."

"She probably felt that she had no choice," Carly said, and reported everything she had learned about Dustin and Era's situation.

"She was hiding him," Luke said. "But I saw him out on the highway once. I gave him and his bicycle and some boxes a ride into town."

"Oh, I saw him in town once, too," Carly recalled. "A few days ago. I remember wondering why he wasn't in school."

"So he didn't always stay hidden." Junior shrugged. "I never saw him. We never had any kind of report or complaint about him. If Era was hiding him, why did she let him come out during the day like that?"

"She may not have known," Carly said, feeling another pang of guilt. "I think she's been sick for a while, probably slept a lot during the day. I know he was out in the neighborhood at night." She told Junior about the disappearing produce and the melons they'd found in Era's refrigerator. "It seems odd that she didn't question where he was getting that food."

"Not if she was sick," Luke pointed out.

They all fell silent for a few seconds.

"He must have had a reason for leaving Waco," Luke said.

"My guess is an uncaring mother. She never followed up after her initial report of his disappearance, although the authorities in Waco kept her up-to-date on anything they found out, which wasn't much." Junior sipped his coffee and stared at the computer screen. "Looks like she's had a series of abusive boyfriends since her husband died. She's filed charges against some of them. Dustin has bounced in and out of foster care."

Carly put her hand to her forehead. "Where do women find guys like that?"

Junior sighed. "Kick over any rock and they just slither out."

"So what's going to happen now?" Luke asked. "Will he go back to his mother?"

"She doesn't want him back. Says she's going to give up her parental rights."

Horrified, Carly stared at him. "What? That's appalling. Why wouldn't she want her son back?"

"I told you. Uncaring mother. She says she can't handle him, wants the state—any state— to take him. He was born in Texas, so they might have jurisdiction, but he's in Oklahoma now, so we'll have to find a foster home to take care of him. We've already called Child Services."

"No. Won't Era want him back?" Carly asked.

"She probably will, but I think it's pretty obvious she can't take care of him, and he's liable to run off again, given his history."

"You don't know that."

Luke gave her a steady look. "He would have run off already if all his clothes weren't in the wash." He stood and went to put Dustin's things in the dryer.

Carly immediately turned to Junior. Purposefully, she set her jaw. "Junior, let me keep him."

"What? Why? You don't know this kid."

"What foster mother does? They're always strangers, and at least I know his grandmother. I knew his dad. You did, too. Joey Salyer? He was a couple of years ahead of us in school. Played football, went into the army and then onto the oil fields for work. That's where he died."

"I remember," Junior said. "It's not up to

me, but from what I've seen on this report, he's pretty hard to handle."

She glanced toward the hallway. "That's probably true," she said, her words dragging with doubts. "But he doesn't need another upheaval, and he loves his grandmother, was trying to take care of her and… I feel guilty because I could have helped him and Era and I didn't. I owe her.

"As soon as his clothes are dry, I'm taking him to see Era, then he could come back here and…stay with me until things get sorted out. Besides, he needs to be in school. He needs normal."

"Carly, you've got to be kidding," Luke said, walking in on the tail of their conversation. He and Junior exchanged the kind of glance that seemed to ask, "What's this woman thinking?"

"No, I'm not kidding." The more she thought about it, the more she knew it was the right thing to do.

Junior considered her for a minute. "Well, I need to get going and I can't take him in his birthday suit. I'll ask Child Services to hold off picking him up until this afternoon.

That'll give you time to think about this. And, they might not even have a placement for him. The county is short on foster homes. Dustin might have to be housed in the county lockup until we find a spot for him."

"Which is his worst fear." She looked from Junior's doubtful face to Luke's grim one. "I've thought about it. This is what I want to do."

"Okay." Junior stood and gathered his things. "I'll tell the sheriff what's going on and call Child Services. They'll be out to talk to you."

"That's fine. That's what I would expect."

She walked Junior out and Luke followed.

As the deputy drove away, Luke asked, "Carly, do you know anything about dealing with troubled kids?"

"I know it won't help to create more trouble for him, put him in jail, drag him away from what little stability he's got, keep him from his grandmother."

"Don't you think you've got enough going on?" With his steady look, he seemed to be trying to get inside her head. "You've got businesses to run and—"

"Natural gas extraction to worry about?" she finished for him. "Yes, I do, but this boy needs help. His mother wants to dump him, for crying out loud. How do you think that's going to make him feel?"

Luke dropped his head forward and shook it, then met her gaze again. "All right, then, I'll help you."

"Help me do what?"

"Look after him."

"I don't need your help. What makes you think you know any more than I do about taking care of a troubled kid?"

He raised an eyebrow and said, "I *don't* know any more than you do, but this is obviously a two-person job. And you'll have to drive him to Toncaville every day to see Mrs. Salyer. I can help with that."

"No." Even if she did know that caring for Dustin would be a struggle, the thought of having Luke around, seeing him every day, caused anxiety to tighten her chest. "I'm the one taking on this responsibility. You don't need to."

"Sure I do." He lifted his hand and moved it in a circling motion. "I'm part of the neighborhood now." He descended the porch steps and said, "In the meantime, I've got to go get my truck. I've got other work to do." With a wave, he headed for his own property. "I'll be back later, and you've got my number, so call if you need me."

Hands on hips, Carly stared after him. She was taking on a runaway boy and, from what she'd seen, he was going to lead her a merry chase. That was hard enough, but now she had a partner she hadn't asked for. It was annoying to realize Luke thought she couldn't do this. Even more annoying to admit she had her own doubts.

Giving a last look at Luke's retreating back, she went into the house to see if any of Dustin's clothes were dry enough for him to get dressed.

CHAPTER TEN

REACHING INTO HIS truck bed, Luke pulled out a case and set it on Carly's porch, then approached the front door. He raised his hand to knock but paused when he heard Carly's voice through the window of the guest room.

"Dustin, you don't have a choice," she said. "You haven't been in school since sometime last spring and you've got to go."

"Why? I hate school. I've been to ten and I hated all of 'em. If I gotta stay with you, then let me work around here. If I wanna learn something, I can read a book or…or I can figure it out myself."

She sighed. "It's true that you've showed real aptitude for picking produce, but you can help me after you've spent a full day at school."

"Ah, come on, dude," Dustin whined.

"Child Services made it very clear that you can only stay here if you're in school."

There was no response from Dustin.

Luke crossed the porch and bent to look in the window. Dustin lay flopped on his bed, staring at the ceiling. Bags from Dyle's Clothing Store were piled beside him. Carly stood over him, clenched fists on her hips, face full of frustration.

"She's right, Dustin. It's the law. You've got to go to school until you turn sixteen."

"That's four *years* from now!" Dustin started and whipped around to see Luke at the window. He propped himself on his elbow and glared. Luke noticed that the boy also had a fresh haircut, so he didn't look quite so much like a wild child.

"That'll give you plenty of time to make your plans to drop out."

"Luke!" Carly gave him an exasperated look. "I thought you were supposed to be helping me here."

Dustin rolled onto his back again, crossed his arms over his chest and resumed his furious examination of the ceiling.

Carly stared at the boy for several seconds while Luke watched emotions flicker across her face—frustration, annoyance and then humor.

She pulled a pair of scissors from her back pocket. "Use these to very carefully cut the tags off your new clothes so we can wash everything."

"I didn't need new clothes. Mine were okay."

"Oh, please, Dustin. The jeans you said were your favorites have more holes than they have denim—which may be fashionable, but not suitable for seventh grade. You can keep them to wear when you help me in the fields."

He didn't respond, so she turned and left the room. Luke stepped back, out of sight, but peeked around the corner. As soon as he thought Carly was gone, Dustin glanced out the window to make sure he was unobserved, then jumped up, dumped the bags out on the bed, and began gleefully holding up shirts and pants, a dark blue hooded sweatshirt and a jacket.

Chuckling to himself, Luke walked away and met Carly at the front door.

"How's Mrs. Salyer?" he asked when she stepped outside.

"Better." Carly hurried across the porch.

"I've got to get to work. I can tell you all about it if you'll… What's that?" she asked, pointing to the large case he'd set on the porch.

"Water testing kit. I've got to check your well."

She shook her head. "Why would you need to check my well?"

"Data collection. I've got to establish a baseline on all the minerals in the water in case…"

"In case you contaminate my well water."

"That's right." He looked at her steadily. There was no point in trying to deny it.

Carly looked tired, but that was no surprise. She'd been up most of the night and spent the day riding herd on an angry boy. Still, she looked beautiful. He let that thought settle into his brain. Yeah, he'd always thought she was beautiful, with her strong profile, full lips and dark brown eyes. That hadn't been what had first attracted him to her, though. It had been her attitude toward life. She had been outgoing and full of plans and ideas. Most of all, she'd been happy. At least, until she'd married him.

"All right. I guess that would be a good

idea." She hurried down the steps and turned toward the shed.

He picked up the kit as he called after her, "It'll only take a few minutes. Then why don't I cook us some dinner?"

Carly rocked to a stop. "Cook dinner?"

"Yeah. I got stuff for hamburgers and a few side dishes from the deli at the Mustang Supermarket. It's in the cooler in the truck. You've got a grill, right?"

"Um, yes." She paused and looked around. "Did I fall down a rabbit hole? Enter an alternate universe? You can cook?"

"Yes, Omi taught me, made me try out recipes. She said she couldn't stand the thought of me eating out every night or having doughnuts for dinner. So, are grilled burgers okay?"

"Yes, okay. That would be nice. I've fed Dustin four times today and he's still hungry. We stopped at the grocery store and loaded up on snacks, and, of course, I've got fields full of food, but he is terrified of being hungry." She shrugged. "Rightly so, I suppose. I'm guessing these past few weeks with his grandmother aren't the first time he's been hungry. He can really pack it away."

"Making up for lost calories. I'll make *big* hamburgers."

Carly shook her head in wonder. "He does dishes and laundry, and he cooks. What a difference twelve years makes."

Luke grinned as he headed for the well.

HE ALSO MADE a mean guacamole, Carly thought as she dipped a tortilla chip into the delicious avocado dip and savored another mouthful. Although the evening was turning chilly, they had decided to eat outside at the picnic table by the grill.

The table was one she'd found at an estate sale, cleaned up and painted a sunny yellow. It was big enough for eight people, far larger than she needed, but the benches had backs on them that could swing up and lock in place, as well as padded cushions. She'd had many offers from people who wanted to buy the set, but she was keeping this one for herself.

They weren't eating by candlelight, but by a row of Mason jars she'd lined up on the table and stuffed with strings of battery-operated fairy lights. A few of them twinkled like trapped fireflies. Dustin seemed mesmerized by them, staring at the jars as he stuffed olives, carrot sticks and tortilla chips into his mouth. She would be worried about him ruining his dinner if she hadn't already seen how much food he could consume at one sitting and be hungry again in twenty minutes.

She was really enjoying this cookout. The only people who cooked for her occasionally were Gemma and Lisa, and now that Gemma was married, she doubted the three of them would be having very many occasions for a girls' night in.

"These burgers will be ready in about five minutes," Luke said as he flipped the hamburger patties and adjusted the flame on the grill. "So, Dustin, tell me how your grandmother is today."

Dustin looked up from the mound of chips he was devouring. "She's okay, I guess. She was awake, and she could talk to me."

"That's good. What did she say?"

Dustin narrowed his eyes as if he couldn't quite believe Luke wanted to have a conversation with him. "That I can stay with Carly."

He held up his hand. "But just till she gets better."

"After she gets out of the hospital, she'll be in a care center for a while, receiving physical therapy," Carly added. "She's very weak. It's going to be a while before she's well."

Luke nodded and changed the subject. "So, you're starting school, when, Dustin?"

After that afternoon's battle, Carly braced herself, but Dustin gave a put-upon sigh and said, "Monday," as if it was a day of doom. "I hate new schools."

Conversation petered out after that. Carly had gone to school in the same district, with the same people, from kindergarten through high school. She had no idea what Dustin had gone through.

After Dustin finished eating, Carly told him he could watch television or a movie.

"I'd rather draw." He jerked his head toward the guest room. "In that pink room," he said, "I saw some paper and stuff."

"Um, sure, Dustin. Help yourself."

He went inside and Carly told Luke, "He was pretty upset when we saw Era at the hospital, but he calmed down when she said she felt better. It'll be a long road until she's well, though."

"Does he know about his mother wanting to hand him over to the state?"

"I don't think so. He didn't ask about her. He's only concerned about his grandmother."

"Since he ran from his mother to his grandmother, I think it's pretty obvious where he wants to be."

Carly nodded, took a sip of her soft drink and said, "Era said she hadn't seen Dustin in two years when he showed up at her door. She hid him, avoided people, so no one would know he was there. She even lied to the deputies, although she said she felt really bad about it. Anyway, she wasn't sure what she was going to do, and then she got sick, started having bouts of vertigo, which meant she couldn't do any of her chores or gardening."

"How'd they survive for four months?"

"Remember the empty canning jars?"

He nodded.

"As we thought, she had quite a stock of frozen and canned food, but they ate it all. Then, of course, Dustin was supplementing their diet with the fresh produce he took from me. She did know what he was doing but couldn't tell me for fear of losing him to his mother or to the state.

"It started in the spring when he brought in some blueberries. She thought I had left them, but when I brought more later that day, she knew Dustin had sneaked out and stolen them. She didn't stop him because she was desperate…and…not thinking right. The bouts of vertigo have been so bad for the past month that she couldn't even drive to town for milk—"

"But you still wish she had called, right?"

"Of course. It hurts that she didn't trust me, but I guess it's understandable if she was afraid someone would take him."

"You're a good neighbor, Carly."

"We all have to look out for each other out here in the country." She paused. "I've never asked, Luke. Where do you live in Dallas?"

"An apartment building. No place special. Why?"

"I just realized that in the past couple of days you've come to learn a lot about my life, but I don't know much about yours."

His grin as he held out his hands was inviting. "Ask away. I'm an open book."

She hesitated because she'd asked a question she shouldn't have asked. It meant she would have to take a step she wasn't ready for. Instead of asking another question, she said, "Apparently you can't tell me what I want to know."

He looked at her for a few seconds then changed the subject. "Your new foster son is quite an enterprising young man, but if Mrs. Salyer hadn't cut her arm, there's no telling what might have happened. On the other hand, if Jay hadn't caught Dustin stealing melons, there's no telling what might have happened."

Carly grimaced. "That crazy plan he and Owen concocted actually saved Era's life. I'll have to tell him tomorrow even though it means he'll never let me forget it."

"Yup."

They fell silent, thinking about everything that had happened in the past twenty-four hours, until Carly said, "Luke, I don't think Era will be able to stay on her own out here. She needs to be in town, so she can get help quickly if she needs it. Even when the infection clears up, and she's had intensive physical therapy, there's still the problem of her vertigo."

"So you might have Dustin for a long time."

"It looks like it."

"You're not thinking of keeping him permanently, are you?"

"After one day? It's a little early for that."

Carly knew that twelve was a rough age, especially for a kid who'd had the kind of life Dustin had, and the tough attitude he showed would probably get worse as he entered his teenage years and tried to find his way. She liked him, though. He loved his grandmother and had been very sweet with her today at the hospital. He was obviously resourceful and he seemed bright. She was hoping, in spite of his sketchy school attendance and all the weeks he'd missed, that he could still be enrolled in the seventh grade to be with kids his own age. Looking after him was going to be tricky, though.

"Carly, there's something else you need to know."

She looked up, meeting Luke's gaze, which

had turned solemn. "My dad is here—at Tom's house. Probably be here for a few days, at least, or until he thinks his office can't run without him. I wanted to let you know in case you ran into him."

Carly's heart had sunk into her gut, but she nodded. "Thanks for telling me. I doubt I'll see him, and I doubt he'd have anything to say to me if I did. Why is he here?"

Luke tilted his head toward his job site. "Still trying to control this project." He told her about Robert's encounter with Shelby, when she'd refused, point-blank, to reveal anything about the process she was developing.

"I wish I'd seen that. She didn't seem very... assertive to me."

"You're no threat to her or what she's working on. Dad is. But apparently she handled it."

"I would have given almost anything to have seen it," Carly said wistfully.

"Me, too."

They exchanged a laughing look and their gazes held. His eyes still crinkled at the corners when he smiled. In another time and another place Robert had been their common irritant, if not their foe.

Luke must have been thinking exactly the same thing because his smile faded into a regretful look and he said, "I'm sorry my dad was always between us."

"He was only one of the obstacles." Carly took a slow, deep breath. Even after all this time, it was hard to talk about it.

"Carly, I—"

"It's okay," she insisted. "There's really nothing to be said after twelve years."

"I disagree."

She surged to her feet. "I've got to get the kitchen cleaned up. There's lots to do. The grand opening of Upcycle is Sunday afternoon and there's a million things to do to get ready."

"I'll help with the dishes. And tomorrow, I'll take Dustin to see his grandmother."

She would have protested, but she realized she was simply too tired to fight.

He left shortly after the kitchen was cleaned up and Carly headed toward her bedroom. She stopped to check on Dustin and found that his room was dark and he was huddled under the covers with one bare foot sticking out. She crossed the room, tucked in his foot, then stood looking down at his face, free of the emotions, mostly anger, that had battered him all day.

She couldn't help thinking about her own child, letting the memory of his tiny face, his shock of black hair, slip out from the place where she kept it locked away. What would he look like now? What kind of person would he be? An even bigger question was what kind of parents would she and Luke have been if they'd managed to overcome their differences and stay together?

That question would never have an answer. They had been too young and too different. And Robert Sanderson had driven too great a wedge between them with his demands that Luke work for him and his insistence that Carly wasn't right for Luke.

And now Luke was back, and so was Robert. If there was any mercy in this world, she wouldn't have to see her former father-in-law, but she couldn't think about that right now. She closed Dustin's door and went to her room.

THIS WAS A busy place on Saturday, Dustin decided. He'd awakened early and, after he got dressed, visited the pantry to load up on food.

Now he was outside exploring. There hadn't been time yesterday since Carly had taken him to see his grandma and then dragged him through the barbershop and the clothing store. She'd even taken him to get the rest of his stuff at Grandma's house. Now, he wanted to look the whole place over. In case he needed to plot escape routes. He'd promised his grandmother he'd stay there, but he never knew when things might change.

Far down one row of the garden, Carly was loading pumpkins into the small trailer she had attached to the back of her four-wheeler. She'd left him a note telling him to get whatever he wanted for breakfast. He didn't have to be told twice. He'd chugged a glass of milk, then grabbed cereal bars, a banana and two packages of toaster pastries, which he'd eaten cold. They weren't as good as Carly's pancakes, but they filled the hole in his gut.

When there hadn't been much food at Grandma's, he'd tried not to think about it. Now that he had plenty of food, he couldn't get enough.

Biting into a cereal bar, he wandered into one of the greenhouses and out again. The tiny seedlings growing in there weren't as interesting as the full-grown veggies outside. He'd been in the gardens before, but not during the day. When he'd been looking for food to take home to Grandma's, or to take into town and sell to the managers at the supermarkets, his visits had always been at night.

That had been okay, until Grandma had gotten sick and he'd been caught by those two dudes. He was still mad about having that giant guy tackle him and slam him to the ground. Dustin's ribs, right knee and cheek still hurt.

The sound of a motorcycle slowing and then pulling into the drive had him turning to see who was coming. His longtime habit of not wanting to be seen before he was ready made him slip behind the oak tree at the corner of the yard and watch the bike and rider who stopped beside Carly's truck. When he stood and pulled off his helmet, Dustin realized it was the dude who had tackled him. Carly had called him Jay.

"Jerk," he muttered.

When the guy went into the shed, he crouched and scurried into the house, then into the pink bedroom. Better to pretend like he was still asleep than to face that guy again. He got out the paper, pencils and pens he'd found in the desk and began drawing what he could see from the window.

One thing he saw was Jay standing in front of Carly, waving his arms and pointing toward the house. Dustin had seen many arguments, many about him, so he suspected that's what this was. After a few minutes, Carly got into her four-wheeler and left the guy standing where he was, shaking his head.

Lost in his art, he didn't hear anyone in the house until someone knocked on his bedroom door. Hastily, he shoved everything into the desk drawer and stood.

"Yeah, come in," he said then waited warily to see who it was.

Of course, it was the last person he wanted to see. "What do you want?" he asked the big dude who filled the doorway.

"Carly said for me to come find you and introduce myself, even though we've already met. My name's Jay Morton."

Dustin didn't say anything. He was busy studying the way the guy stood, blocking the way out. Dustin instantly decided he could go through the window if he needed to, but he wasn't sure what his chances were of getting away since he already knew how fast this guy could move.

Jay looked him over and Dustin straightened, wanting to make himself look as big as possible.

"She says you need to get up and come outside."

"I'm up."

"Then come outside." Jay stepped back, but Dustin moved around him warily, never actually turning his back to the big teenager.

"You should know, though, that I'll be watching you. I think Carly's making a big mistake keeping you here, but she wants to help Mrs. Salyer. I think you're a thief and a sneak, so I'll be watching you," Jay repeated.

"Yeah, I heard you the first time." Dustin finally turned his back on Jay and hurried out the front door, putting as much distance as possible between them.

Carly drove up to them and gave them both a wide smile. "Good morning, Dustin. Did you get some breakfast?"

"Yeah, so what if I did?"

"Hey!" Jay yelped. "Don't be dissing her, you little punk."

Dustin scowled at him as Carly appeared to bite her tongue and continue. "So, if you've had breakfast, that means you can help out at the produce stand today. Halloween is coming and we want people to buy their pumpkins from us. Sheena can't come in today because she's sick, so I'm recruiting you to help."

Dustin wrinkled his nose. "Nah, I don't wanna work at a—"

"I'll pay you, of course."

He stopped and looked at her. He liked money. He'd gotten a little from selling the produce he'd borrowed from Carly's gardens, but in the past, he'd mostly taken it from his mom's purse. Maybe earning it would be better.

"How much?" He nodded toward Jay. "I want as much as he makes."

Jay made a sound of disgust but before he could say anything, Carly went on. "I can't pay you as much as Jay makes because he has experience."

"*He's* got experience," Jay pointed out. "At least in picking produce."

"Jay," she cautioned and then looked back at Dustin. "Five dollars an hour, and you'll earn raises as you learn how to do the various jobs around here, but you really have to work, not stand around or disappear."

Dustin thought about it. It sounded good to him, but he didn't want to seem too eager, especially with his enemy standing there, watching and listening. At last he said, "Okay, then. What do I have to do?"

She gave him a brilliant smile, like she was actually glad to have his help. It made him feel weird inside. He had to remind himself that he'd taken stuff from her to help his grandma, not because he'd wanted to. Not because he was a real thief—not like some people said.

"We're already getting a late start so I want us to get the stand open as fast as we can." She waved a hand toward the four-wheeler. "I've picked the last of the melons and some pumpkins. We'll take those down to the stand and you can open up, start helping customers. Do you know how to make change?"

He shrugged. "I dunno. I guess."

"I'll show you."

"You're gonna trust him with the cash box?" Jay squawked.

"I ain't a thief!" Dustin yelled.

"Yeah, right."

"I was gonna pay for what I took."

"Uh-huh," Jay said.

That skeptical attitude only made Dustin madder. "You remember that note I left when you were trying to catch me but you fell asleep and your snoring scared all the animals?"

"Hey!"

"Well, on the back, I was keeping track of everything I harvested so I could pay for it."

"Harvested, huh? Well, it's time for you to start paying, but I don't know why Carly wants to hire you."

"Jay," Carly said, "this is my decision, and my business. Why don't you go get the other four-wheeler and start picking more pump-kins?"

Dustin was happy to see she was getting mad, but not at him.

Jay gave a wave of his hand as he stomped off. "Whatever."

He looked up at Carly. "I've gotta go in the house a minute, then you can show me what I hafta do." He ran inside. This was going to be epic, he thought, but he had to be quick.

CARLY GAVE DUSTIN a dubious look. He was suddenly way too happy about helping her out, and she really hoped it wasn't a terrible mistake to give him the cash box. Still, what was he going to do? Tuck it under his arm and run down the road? Besides, she needed to begin building trust with him sooner rather than later.

"Dustin, I'm believing in you to do your best and to be completely honest," she said as they lined up the pumpkins on top of the counter.

"I will." He gave a nod, even a smile.

This was the most cooperative he'd been since she'd met him.

She showed him how to make change, then he helped her affix the sign advertising the pumpkins on each side of the booth so drivers could see it whether they were heading north or south.

"I find it's easier to sell these if I go by size rather than weight, so we set prices by small, medium and large. People around here don't care how much it weighs, they mostly want a certain size jack-o'-lantern. And don't try and lift the largest ones. Let the buyers do that."

"I can do it," he insisted. "I'm strong."

Seeing she'd hurt his feelings, she quickly said, "I know you are, Dustin. I don't want you to get hurt."

"I won't." He looked away sullenly.

"Okay, okay." She pulled a ledger from beneath the counter. "I like to keep a record of how many I sell each year, so that I know how much to plant next year. So, when you sell one, make a tally mark and we'll add them up at the end of the day."

"Wouldn't it be easier to do this on a computer?"

"Probably, but we're only making tally marks right now."

"So, when do I get paid?"

"Every Friday."

"I gotta wait almost a *week*?" He gave her

a put-upon look. "You're gonna take me to see Grandma today, right? I wanna buy her some flowers."

Touched by his thoughtfulness, even if he only showed it to one person on earth, she said, "Oh, of course. That would be nice. I'll pay you before we go." Carly looked toward the four-wheeler and thought about all the work that needed to be done before she could go into town. "So, you'll be okay here, right?"

"Yeah. I'll be okay." He turned away, rubbing his hands together and then cracking his knuckles as if he was getting ready for a big job.

Something about the way he said it made her nervous, but she closely observed his face for a few seconds and decided it would be all right. Besides, she needed his help, and Jay would be here pretty soon with more pumpkins.

Less than half an hour later, she glanced toward the road and saw that several cars had stopped. Dustin must be doing a good job of selling. Maybe she would give him a bonus before she took him to see Era. He might like to get a little gift for her.

A few minutes later she was coming out of the shed with the wheelbarrow when Luke pulled up in his truck. She gave him a quick glance then looked again when it seemed he was struggling to get his door open. At last, it flew outward and he tumbled out, barely catching himself from falling. He was laughing so hard, he could barely stand.

"Luke, what's going on?"

"You...*hoov*...you've got to see...see this." He bent at the waist to catch his breath and wiped tears of laughter from his eyes.

"See what? Are you okay?"

"Yeah, yeah, but things are going to get pretty hot in a minute. And, yeah, I know, I shouldn't be laughing about this."

"About what? Luke, what are you talking about?" She stared at him in frustration. In spite of his amusement, she had a bad feeling. "Luke, answer me."

He pointed up the lane, where Jay was driving toward the road, hauling more pumpkins out to the stand in the small trailer attached to the four-wheeler. "Too late. I don't think we can head him off."

That didn't sound good. She dropped the handles of the wheelbarrow. "What's going on?"

"Get in the truck," he instructed. "You need to get down to the produce stand."

"Why? I can walk there."

"Too slow," he said, dashing around the front of the truck and opening the passenger door for her.

She scrambled inside and he burned gravel as he made a 180-degree turn to follow Jay.

Luke sat forward in the seat, leaning over the steering wheel. "We can't get ahead of him, but at least we'll arrive at the stand when he does."

"Why would we need to?"

"Just wait. I'd tell you, but I want you to get the full impact."

That *really* didn't sound good.

Luke was trying desperately to keep his expression under control. Puzzled, she stared ahead to see that Dustin had made a few changes to the signs on the produce stand. He'd turned them around and written new ones in thick black marker.

Out loud, she read, "'$8—Pumpkins as big as Jay Morton's butt. $6—Pumpkins as big as Jay Morton's head. $4—Pumpkins as small as Jay Morton's...' Oh, my goodness! Dustin!"

CHAPTER ELEVEN

SHE JERKED UP the door handle at the exact moment Jay let out a howl of outrage.

"You little scum," he yelled, jumping off his vehicle. "I'll kill you."

"Jay, stop!" Carly shrieked. "Luke, help me!"

Luke was already ahead of her, running to get between the two boys. He held out his arms to prevent Jay from reaching Dustin, who was laughing uproariously. That only infuriated Jay even more.

"Get out of the way, Mr. Sanderson. Let me get at him so I can kill him." Jay made a grab for the younger boy, but Luke blocked it. "If I bury his body in the woods, nobody will ever know."

"No, Jay, calm down," Luke insisted.

Carly put a soothing hand on Jay's arm, and that's when she spied the pumpkins lined up on the counter. Her mouth dropped open.

The orange vegetables were now decorated

with faces—obviously Jay's face in different guises—drawn in the same black marker. In one he was depicted as a popular cartoon bad guy who had a swoop of hair that stood straight up from his head. In another he was a sad-eyed elephant. In the next he was depicted as Elvis Presley.

"I had more," Dustin said proudly. "But I sold 'em. Jay Buttface will be all over town."

"Aaaah!" Jay yelled, incoherent with rage as he tried to make a grab for Dustin, who skipped behind the counter and picked up one of the smaller pumpkins to defend himself. Jay made more swipes for him, but Luke blocked all of his threatening moves, finally grabbing one wrist, spinning him around and holding on to his upper arms.

While all of this was going on, a couple of cars slowed down, looked at what was going on, and drove off with the occupants laughing.

"Dustin, turn those signs around," Luke ordered, still holding Jay's arms. "And put those pumpkins out of sight."

"Ah, come on," the boy protested. "It was just a joke."

"Now." Luke gave him a steely-eyed look, and Dustin did as he said, although Carly had to help him lift the biggest pumpkins from the counter and replace them with undecorated ones. She tilted one back and stared in wonder at the perfection of the drawing, however inappropriate it was. This kid had natural talent. Misdirected, but brilliant.

"Dustin, I can't believe you did that," Carly said, shaking her head. "Why would you write…"

"'Cause he's a jerk."

"You're about to find out how much of a jerk I can be," Jay yelled. He wasn't calming down at all.

Luke looked over at Carly and said, "The best thing we can do right now is separate them."

"I wanna separate him from his head!" When Jay managed to twist away from Luke, Dustin skipped behind Carly.

She quickly turned and said, "Dustin, you go up to the house and stay in your room until I get there to talk to you. And I'd better not have to come find you. If you run away, I'll have to call Child Services and you'll be taken to a real foster home. Maybe far away from your grandmother, which is something that none of us want."

Anger, followed by fear, flared in his eyes. She hated having to say that to him, but it might be the only way to get his attention.

Without another word, he turned and ran for the house.

She sent a worried look after him then turned to Jay. "I know this is all about the other night when you tackled him, but it doesn't help that you keep calling him a thief."

"You think this is *my* fault?"

"You share in the blame, and you have to own it," Luke said.

"No way. If that kid can't handle the truth, he can stay out of my sight." He stomped angrily back to the four-wheeler and began unloading pumpkins, stopping only to glare at the ones Dustin had decorated. He snatched them up and threw them in the trailer. Carly started to protest his rough treatment of produce, but Luke put his hand on her arm to stop her. When Jay was finished, he left without a word, gunning the motor of his vehicle.

Luke started to say something but she held up her hand. "Don't remind me that you said I shouldn't take Dustin, and don't tell me I'm not handling this well. I'm doing my best."

He held up his hands, all innocence. "I didn't say—"

"And didn't you volunteer to help me with Dustin?"

He gave her a wary look. "Of course."

"Laughing at this—" she gestured at the offensive signs "—isn't helping."

"Maybe not, but did you see the faces on the pumpkins? Dead on!" He joined her behind the counter. "Did you get a good look at the Elvis one? Unbelievable."

Carly bit her lip to keep from laughing.

"If Dustin would decorate these other pumpkins with faces, or animals, ghosts and goblins, people would pay more for them. In fact, people could custom order what they want."

"People like to carve their own pumpkins," she pointed out.

"No, they really don't. It's messy and they never look good unless you've got one of those patterns to follow and a sharp knife.

You want to put a sharp knife in that kid's hand?"

"Um, well, no." She paused. "Where did you learn so much about pumpkin carving?"

He shrugged. "One of Omi's community center projects a couple of years ago. I was in charge of jack-o'-lantern creation. Believe me when I say people always think that's what they want, but the messy reality is different. The kids might start the project, but they don't like touching the slimy stuff inside the pumpkin and the mom of the family ends up doing it all. That's why we need to get Dustin to paint faces on pumpkins. The moms of Reston will thank you."

"Have you never heard of child labor laws?"

"You're the one who had him working here. Might as well take advantage of his…productivity."

"You think we should reward him for what he did?"

"No, I think he should apologize for what he did, and then you propose that he turn this into a real money-maker, with the condition that you help him set up a bank account and he saves most of the money."

Carly thought it over. "It would give him more incentive to stay…"

"And make it harder for him to leave if most of his money is tied up in the Reston Savings Bank."

"You realize we're talking about him as if he's much older than twelve."

"Only his chronological age is twelve. His years of street smarts put him in the geriatric category."

She nodded. "That's sadly true."

"Admit it, Carly. You know that putting him to work is a good idea—especially on something he obviously has a talent for. See, I said I'd help you. This is helpful."

She considered him for a second. "Fine, I'll talk to him about it, but he has to apologize to Jay first, and make an effort to get along with him. And Jay will have to do the same thing." She started for the house. "And since you're so eager to help, you can man this booth while I talk to them both. The cash box is under the counter. Keep a tally of everything you sell. I use the sales results to plan my planting for next spring."

"Hey," he objected. "I've got to finish fixing the fence. I do have another job, you know."

"You probably should have thought of that before offering to get involved with a troubled kid who's smarter than both of us."

CARLY PAUSED OUTSIDE Dustin's door. She wasn't sure what to say. Her experience with kids, especially middle school–aged boys, was nonexistent. Hoping that the right words would come at the right time, she knocked on the door.

"Yeah, come in," Dustin responded.

He was sitting at the desk and he quickly flipped over the paper in front of him so she couldn't see it. That was fine with her. She had no desire to see what he was drawing now.

"What you did to Jay wasn't very nice, and I think you know that. You need to apologize."

He glared at her. "Him first. What he did to me wasn't very nice, either." He pointed to his fading bruise. "He coulda killed me."

"That's an exaggeration."

"Yeah, let him knock *you* down, then."

"Dustin, there's no reason to be rude to me."

He looked away but didn't apologize.

Carly took a deep breath then let it out slowly and said, "In spite of your attitude, Luke has come up with a money-making idea for you."

He looked up, eyes alert. "Yeah, what?"

"Well, that got your attention." She told him about Luke's suggestion for creating jack-o'-lanterns. "But first, you have to say sorry to Jay, and he'll say sorry to you."

He considered it. "Okay, but I get to keep all the money I earn, right?"

She didn't even have to think about that one. There was no way she was giving this kid traveling money. "Most of it will go in the bank."

"What?" He jumped up, ready to argue.

"You might need it someday to help your grandma," she said, grasping at straws.

Her desperate gamble paid off and he nodded. Dustin sat again and returned to drawing.

Realizing she'd been dismissed, Carly left

the room and stood in the hallway. She'd known taking Dustin in would be hard, but she hadn't known how hard. She thought of all the impossibly difficult challenges she'd faced in the past twelve years. None of them compared to Dustin.

Taking another deep breath, she went back to work.

"I SHOULD HAVE known better than to turn Lisa and Gemma loose on food and decorations," Carly murmured. The large barnwood table had been moved to the middle of the shop and decorated with bright orange placemats, bowls of brilliant maple leaves, platters of food, small sandwiches, crudités and other finger foods. "Especially since Sunshine is back in town for a while, bringing recipes from countries she's visited all over the world."

Gemma swept up to look over the offerings on the loaded table. "Did I hear my mom's name taken in vain?" she asked.

"Not a chance. You know how much I love your mom. But some of the things she brought back with her..." Carly said dubiously. "Do you really think we can get the people of Reston to try yak butter?"

"Yes, I do. We'll tell them it's been specially imported as a condiment for the meat pies donated by Margie's Kitchen—guaranteed to help them slide down and stay down."

"Hmm, might be a dubious selling point, but we'll go with what we have," Lisa said as she walked by with a tray of soft drinks. She needed to find a place where it would be protected from overeager children. Spying a tall industrial shelving unit that Carly had sandblasted, spray-painted red and decorated with replicas of old-fashioned oil-and-gas-themed stickers, she decided it would be the best place for the drinks.

Carly marveled at how her friend could perfectly balance those drinks while wearing high-heeled pumps and a snug skirt. Practice, she decided. Lisa dressed up every day. Gemma, on the other hand, had worn jeans, a T-shirt and sneakers, as Carly had, knowing they would have to move stock and help carry sold items out to customers' vehicles. Nathan would be along later to help, as well. Carly chuckled to herself. No one would expect a woman dressed like Lisa to haul furniture.

At ten minutes before the grand opening, Carly, her friends, both her employees and even Jay, slightly less sullen today, made a quick turn around the shop.

Janie, one of the employees, said, "If we're lucky, we can probably sell a bunch of stock today. A big grand opening is like a feeding frenzy. People buy things before they're really sure they need them because they're afraid they'll miss a deal or a one-of-a-kind piece. And everything at Upcycle is one of a kind. I emailed some of Carly's customers from Dallas. Several said they'd like to come up since it's a nice Sunday afternoon."

"Oh, joy," Carly murmured. "A feeding frenzy."

"And a Helen Voller called about the Hoosier cabinet." Janie pointed across the room to the old-fashioned sideboard Carly had chalk-painted in sky blue. "She saw it on the website, bought it and will be here to pick it up this afternoon."

Across the room, Lisa cleared her throat loudly and when Carly looked at her, she blew on her hot-pink fingernails and buffed them proudly against her dress.

Carly wrinkled her nose at her friend. "Yeah, yeah, the website was your idea and it's great."

"Just so you remember who to thank," Lisa responded.

Carly turned away, smiling as she surveyed all they'd done. She'd fought the idea of the shop because of her fear of failing, of disappointing someone, or herself, but those fears were unfounded. With this much help, she knew she could handle the frantically busy day and the ones to come.

She walked to the front window and looked out to where Luke and Dustin were setting up a display of the jack-o'-lanterns Dustin had created. He'd even hand-printed a neatly lettered sign promising that his artistic Halloween decorations would last far longer than carved ones. His display would crowd the sidewalk in front of the store, but having him involved in a positive activity would be worth it.

Lisa and Gemma joined her at the window.

"So," Gemma said, drawing out the word. "Luke is around…"

"A lot," Lisa added. "What's up with that?"

"Darned if I know," Carly answered. "But he's been helping me with Dustin—which actually *has* been helpful."

Looking around furtively to see where Jay was, she told them about yesterday's craziness. They both laughed and even Carly cracked a smile. "It wasn't funny at the time."

"So, Dustin's new artistic enterprise was Luke's idea?" Gemma asked.

"That's right."

Gemma and Lisa exchanged a look and Lisa said, "Well, that's fine as long as he's being useful." She held a warning finger in the air. "But, if he hurts you again…" Lisa linked arms with her on the right side, as Gemma did on the left.

"I know. I know. He could disappear out in the woods where no one would ever find him."

"Not that we would *ever* resort to violence," Gemma added innocently. "We just want you to know we've got your back."

They all three laughed.

"I can't believe how talented that kid is," Lisa said, changing the subject. "And how good he is at marketing."

Gemma chuckled. "Maybe you should hire him to help you sell houses."

"There's an idea. Maybe he can turn your husband's old family home into a haunted house, see if we can attract the ghoulish crowd."

Gemma shook her head. "No, all those unhappy old ghosts are gone. You'll find a buyer. We're not worried."

The three of them watched Dustin directing Luke where to place his handiwork so it would get the most exposure. Thank fortune, the theatrics at the gardens had settled down. Dustin had apologized to Jay. The older boy had accepted his apology and said he was sorry, too. Although she knew neither apology was sincere, at least the warring factions had called a truce. She wasn't sure how long it would hold.

Dustin had been delighted at the idea of decorating pumpkins and earning a commission on the ones that sold. He had set to work right away. She was amazed at how quickly he could look at a photograph and transform a pumpkin into the likeness of an animal. He'd come up with his own renditions of goblins, telling Carly he mostly based them on his mother's old boyfriends.

She said this out loud to Gemma and Lisa.

"I can't imagine what that kid has been through," she added.

"Have you told him yet that his mother wants to give him up, turn him over to the state?" Lisa asked. "I know what it's like to have a mother who doesn't want you."

Carly put her arm around Lisa's shoulders. "I talked it over with Era, and we're looking for the right time to tell him."

Out of the corner of her eye, she saw Jay disappear into the back room and hoped he hadn't heard. She couldn't worry about it now. It was time to open.

Walking to the front door, she flipped the lock and welcomed her first customers.

As expected, the store was frantically busy all afternoon. Carly even sold the barn-wood table that held the refreshments to Luke's cousin, Trent Sanderson, and his wife, Mia, who had come in with Tom and Frances.

Baby Max eagerly tried to grasp whatever he could reach until Trent hoisted him onto his shoulders and held him in place with a hand on each of his chubby thighs. Mia claimed the table immediately, saying it was perfect for their new house. They would pick it up after closing time.

At some point Dustin had sold all his pumpkins and began taking special orders. She only hoped his enterprise would meet with the approval of Child Services. She also hoped he didn't sell out her entire stock of pumpkins and there would be some left for the Reston Elementary kindergarteners.

During a momentary lull in the stream of customers and well-wishers, Lisa stopped next to her and grabbed a bottle of water. "I know what you're happiest about in all this."

"You do? Enlighten me."

"You're happiest that you can go out and find more junk—"

"Well-used and well-loved items," Carly objected.

Lisa laughed. "Whatever you call it. You're just happy to find more stuff to rescue and refurbish."

"Why, you're absolutely right. And may I remind you that this shop was your idea so I could clear out my stock and make use of an empty shop in town, not to mention attracting visitors and business to Reston."

"I didn't know my own strength," Lisa muttered mournfully. "I've created a monster."

Laughing, Carly turned away and came face-to-face with Robert Sanderson. She hadn't seen him in twelve years, but she certainly hadn't forgotten what he looked like—tall, imposing, dark hair going gray and the same caramel-brown eyes that Luke had, though his were more somber and secretive. She'd never had to wonder what Robert was thinking, because he'd made no secret of his disappointment that his son had married her—a nobody, someone who couldn't possibly give his son any social or business advantage.

At the time, she'd felt stupidly guilty about her modest upbringing, but now she had to wonder what century he came from.

Her heart plummeted into her stomach and she knew her welcoming smile was shaky as she said, "Hello, Robert. Welcome to Up-cycle."

"Carly," he said with a nod. He began strolling around.

She immediately felt Gemma and Lisa at her back, but the one she saw was Luke. He came in the door, his gaze seeking her out, his smile brightening and then fading when he spotted his father.

He hurried to Robert's side. "Dad. What are you doing here?"

Robert raised his eyebrows. "Shopping."

"Whatever for?"

Carly knew he was trying and failing to imagine any of her cast-off, upgraded and brightly painted stock in his father's deliber-ately neutral house.

"This right here," he said, putting his hand on the bright red shelving unit. "It's avail-able, right?"

"Yes, sir," Carly answered.

"Don't say 'sir,'" Lisa hissed under her breath. "That implies respect."

Carly elbowed her.

Robert took out his wallet. "Okay if we transport it in your truck, son?"

"Where are we taking it?"

"Dr. Wayne's workroom."

"You're kidding."

"Not at all. She needs a shelf for her equipment. This will work."

Robert looked up with that expression Carly remembered all too well, as if he expected his wishes to be instantly granted. She looked at Luke, expecting to see the response he'd always shown his father, exasperated compliance.

This time, he surprised her by giving his dad a narrow-eyed look and saying, "Dad, can I talk to you outside for a moment?"

Although he looked taken aback, Robert said, "Certainly," as he handed his credit card to Carly.

Luke jerked the door open and waved his father out. They stepped away from the entrance.

"Wow," Gemma murmured. "I'd love to hear what they're saying."

"Darn," Lisa said, moving closer to the window and craning her neck to see where the two men had gone. "Why didn't I ever learn to read lips?"

Carly looked down at the card.

"'Robert L. Sanderson,'" Gemma read. "What does the *L* stand for?"

"Lucifer?" Lisa suggested.

The three of them snickered, but Carly grew solemn. "It stands for Luke."

She slipped the card into her pocket. She wouldn't run it until she understood what was going on between Luke and his father. Not that she had ever understood. She glanced out to see Dustin busily working on his pumpkins, then turned to talk to her customers.

"DAD, IS THIS your latest attempt to weasel your way into controlling my project?"

"Weasel! That's some way to talk to your father." Robert's face stiffened with rage.

"I'm not talking to my father right now. I'm talking to a man who won't trust me to do a job I'm qualified to do." It wasn't the first time this had happened, but for some reason, it was the most infuriating. He'd known his dad couldn't leave this alone, but he'd expected pestering phone calls, demands for reports, not an in-person visit.

"I'm keeping an eye on my investment."

"It looks like you were buying a shelving unit for Shelby so you'll have a reason to visit the site again."

"I stopped by the site to say hello. She said she needs shelves and I know she's not the kind of person who wants her equipment scattered all over the floor."

"If she needs shelves, *I'll* buy them. You promised me another six months before you'd start poking your nose in, and yet, here you are."

"I'm not planning to lose any money on this." Robert glanced away.

"You haven't actually put any money into it, Dad, and you know that. Besides, you know I'll do everything I can to make sure this project succeeds." Luke held his ground. "What's this really about?"

Robert swept aside the sides of his jacket and stood with his hands on his hips. "I didn't think you'd be fool enough to take up with her again."

"Take up with… You mean Carly?" Luke jerked his thumb back toward the entrance to Upcycle. "I should *be* so lucky."

"What?" To Luke's astonishment, his father's face actually paled. "What do you mean, Luke?"

"After what happened between us, the way I hurt her, let you hurt her, Carly wouldn't have me if I came dipped in solid gold." It made his gut clench to say it out loud, but he knew it was true.

His dad opened and closed his mouth a couple of times. Luke took a perverse pleasure in seeing his father at a loss for words. "But…but that was twelve years ago. She… she would have forgotten."

"No, Dad. That's not the kind of thing she would forget. If I'm lucky, someday, maybe, she might forgive me, but she'll never forget. And I know exactly how long it's been. I've lived every day of it."

"The more you're around her, the more you'll want to *be* around her. It's a slippery slope."

"She needs my help, Dad, and, after all this time, I'm glad I can help her."

"You'll get caught up in her life, in her business—"

"I already am."

"Tom says you're helping her with that kid

she's taken in." Robert made a gesture that encompassed the area. "I know you're helping with all of this because you feel guilty."

"Yes, I do, and you should, too."

When Robert didn't respond, Luke said, "I'll buy the shelves for Shelby. Wait here. I'll get your credit card from Carly. I'm sure she didn't run it. I doubt that she wants your money. She probably doesn't want mine, either."

He hurried inside and asked for Robert's card, which Carly handed over without a word but with a sympathetic smile.

When he returned it, Robert put it back in his wallet, got into his car and drove away, leaving Luke with the frustrated, empty feeling he almost always experienced when dealing with his dad. It never got better and he didn't think it would ever change.

He bought the shelving unit, had Jay help him load it into his truck, then returned to his job of supervising Dustin, who, temporarily at least, had found his niche.

CARLY FLIPPED THE empty pizza box into the trash. Even after snacking all day, the crew had been hungry. They had pulled up her assortment of chairs to the barn-wood table and devoured the pizza she'd ordered. Trent and Tom would be along to pick up the table soon, but the crew was in no hurry to clear up the last of the mess and get the store ready for tomorrow.

"Looks like you're off and running," Luke said. He held up his can of soda. "To Carly and to Upcycle."

Everyone else joined in and she smiled as she toasted them back. "And to all of my wonderful friends. Thank you from the bottom of my heart."

Gemma's phone pinged and she glanced at the display, then looked up, green eyes shining. "Karina Parks is in labor. I've got to go."

Nathan stood with her. "I'll come, too."

Gemma gave him a smile. There had been a time only a few months ago when he would have insisted on accompanying her because he thought midwives were incompetent. However, he had learned to trust her and they had worked through tough issues to reach the mutual confidence and love they now enjoyed.

Carly was happy for them but also a little

jealous. They worked together, had each other's backs, believed in and depended on each other. It was a pleasure to be near them.

Gemma and Nathan quickly gathered their things and left. No matter how long this night was, how difficult the birth, they would be together at every step.

Her employees finished the last chores and headed home, leaving only her, Dustin, Luke and Lisa, who was in the back room, washing up the last of the nondisposable dishes they'd used.

Dustin spied a vintage checkers set and began putting out the pieces.

Carly picked up a large binder and began jotting down some notes.

Luke walked up behind her and looked over her shoulder. "What's this?"

She opened the book wider so he could see. "It's how I keep inventory."

"Before-and-after pictures of the pieces in the shop?"

"Yes. When I sell a piece, I add a note about the buyer if I know their name. Then, if I get something similar that they might like,

I can call them. Or, since I now have a website, I can contact them that way."

"Will my name be in there for buying the shelving unit?"

He was much too close. She could feel his warmth against her shoulder, the slight puff of his breath against her hair. For some ridiculous reason, she felt heat rush into her face as she turned to meet his gaze. Those caramel-brown eyes warmed with his smile as she said, "Of course."

It would be so easy to lean forward just a bit and place her lips on his. He wasn't that much taller than her. It wouldn't take much effort at all. She hadn't kissed him in many, many years, and it was such a sweet memory. Her heart did a slow, soft roll in her chest as she drank in the warmth and humor in his eyes. She leaned in the tiniest bit.

"Oh, Carly, inventory tonight? Aren't you exhausted?" Lisa walked up with her purse on her shoulder and an empty, clean dish in her hand. She was still examining it for any offending spots.

Carly and Luke sprang apart and she tried to focus on what her friend had asked.

"Um, well, yeah, I'm tired, but I've got to see what I need to bring in to fill in my stock. Since Tom and Trent picked up the dining set, I've got room for more. Fall brush and bulky pick up begins next week and—"

"Oh, no," Lisa groaned.

"Brush and bulky?" Luke asked. "What is that?"

Lisa smiled fondly at her friend. "That's one of the two times a year the good people of Reston County can put out items they need to discard like yard clippings and tree branches that they can't burn. Also, items that are too big to fit in their bins. The highways and by-ways are littered with cast-off furniture, appliances, chairs, tables, you name it. Brush and bulky pickup is also known as Carly Visits Heaven Week. She's in her element, spends the whole time out, digging through other people's junk. She's like a windup toy that never winds down."

Carly, who had continued with her inventory while Lisa talked, looked back and said, "And that's where I get the stock for this shop you insisted I open."

"I know. I already admitted that I've helped create a monster."

"It's an exaggeration to say I collect everything. I draw the line at upholstered furniture found on the side of the road."

"Too dirty?" Luke asked.

"Too many places for critters to hide, including snakes."

Luke raised an eyebrow. "I'd think you'd have dealt with lots of snakes in your gardens."

"I have. That's why I don't want to find them in furniture."

From across the room, Dustin asked, "Luke, do you know how to play checkers?"

"Oh," Carly said. "I'm sorry, Dustin, I'd forgotten you're still here. You need to get home and to bed. Your first day of school is tomorrow." She put down her clipboard. "Which means inventory can wait."

"Aw, Carly," he said. "Just one game."

She shook her head. "No game. At least, not tonight. We can take the set home, though, and you and Luke can have a game another time."

Luke gave her a surprised look as she turned away to gather her things and lock up the shop.

"Sure, Dustin, I can do that," he said. "How about tomorrow after school?"

Dustin shrugged. "Okay."

They all trooped outside and she locked up.

Luke waited to leave until she and Dustin were in her truck and headed home.

LUKE STARTED HIS truck and drove toward Frances and Tom's house.

Every word he'd said to his dad was true. He was lucky that Carly had let him back into her life if only in a small way—even if she couldn't trust his plans for the extraction operation, and even if he still felt guilty about what had happened between them.

When he stopped at a traffic sign, he rubbed his chin thoughtfully. He understood Carly's reluctance to trust him, and her wariness around his father, but there had been something in her attitude toward Robert, and in Robert's attitude toward her, that he couldn't quite decipher, as if their mutual dislike also included…guilt.

Nah. He'd misread it because he'd had guilt and forgiveness on his mind so much lately.

His thoughts returned to Carly. He was

proud of the person she'd become, of what she'd accomplished. He tried to think back to when they'd met, when they'd married in a rush. He'd been proud of her looks, her wit, her sunny nature, but had he ever showed pride in what she'd done? In the 3.75 grade point average she'd achieved at university? He couldn't recall, which meant he hadn't.

Since the day she'd left him, she had worked hard to succeed on her own. She'd created an entire life without him, one that included community, family and friends. Lisa and Gemma had each given him the I'm-watching-you gesture at least twice today. He knew other people were watching him, as well, including his own aunt and uncle. They wanted to be sure history didn't repeat itself.

Luke had created a new life for himself, as well, but it had included a lengthy avoidance of his father while he'd worked on construction projects and oil fields in South America. When he'd returned to Dallas to be near Omi, he'd created another life, but it didn't have the richness of Carly's—the life she was temporarily sharing with Dustin.

Luke was a small part of it because they

were working together to help Dustin. If and when Dustin went back to his grandmother, the only things between them would be the past and the oil extraction process. In other words, unhappy memories and the possibility of harming her land, her livelihood, her. Again.

CHAPTER TWELVE

"IF YOU GET lost or confused, just ask some-one for help," Carly advised.

Dustin glanced at her with an overdone eye roll. He had refused to let Carly walk him to his first class. The school wasn't all that big. It was attached to the high school, which wasn't very big, either. He could find his own way, and he'd had enough of foster moms taking him to class and warning the teacher that he was a troublemaker. One of them had gone so far as to turn to the class and advise them to tell on him if he caused any trouble. He'd been in four fights that day, which meant he'd been suspended and the foster mom had had to keep him home. He'd only been at that place for three more days. Couldn't even re-member those people's names.

He didn't think Carly would do anything to humiliate him, but still, here he was again starting at his eleventh school. Mostly, she was cool and living with her kept him close to his grandma, the one person in the world who was glad he was alive. And Carly paid him for his work. He *really* liked having his own money. Too bad she was also going to make him put it in the bank. She did let him keep a little of it, though.

Dustin looked down at his new shoes, new jeans, new shirt, new hoodie, then at the new backpack in his hand. This stuff screamed, "Bully me." He liked the new stuff, but he hated being the new kid.

He also hated that he couldn't do anything about it. The law said he had to go to school and now that his grandma felt better she was determined to follow the law. He wasn't sure what had changed, but she didn't seem worried about Texas Rangers showing up to clap him in handcuffs and take him back to Waco. Was that what Texas Rangers did? Either way, they were tough and only the toughest could take him in.

"Don't worry, Dustin," she said. "You'll be fine."

"Like you'd know," he muttered.

"What?" she asked, putting her hand on

his shoulder and bending close, like he was a kindergartener.

"Nothing. Look, I'd better go." He shook her off and headed for the front door. He'd figure this out. He always did. For some baby reason, he looked back at Carly. She *was* cool, even if she was only letting him live with her because she was friends with Grandma. And Luke was cool. Only Jay was a jerk.

Surreptitiously he looked down at the paper in his hand to double-check the room number. The secretary in the office had showed him and Carly where to go, and he'd met the teacher, Mrs. Dobbins, earlier. Now he had to walk into a roomful of staring faces.

He hesitated with his hand on the knob, then twisted it and walked in. Sure enough, every face turned to him, including the one belonging to a big kid with mean, piggy eyes that lit up when he saw Dustin.

Oh, yeah. There was always one of those.

WITH SHELBY'S HELP, Luke moved the shelving unit into her workspace, then had to wave away her thanks and admit it had been his dad's idea. She began happily storing her supplies and he took himself off to finish the fence he and Carly had started days ago.

As he pulled on his gloves, strung and stapled the barbed wire, he thought about everything that had happened since he'd pulled into Carly's driveway on Memorial Day to deliver his grandmother's trunk. He hadn't expected to see her again, except possibly from a distance. Yet here he was, seeing her almost every day, helping her ride herd on the imaginative and irrepressible Dustin. Repairing her fence.

He'd been thinking about this constantly since last night.

He frowned. The fence that separated their properties was nothing compared to the chasm between them. When he'd thought he'd never see her again, it hadn't bothered him so much. He'd buried it. Now, though, seeing her all the time, having his father suspicious that he was going to get back together with her, made him think about what had happened between them and how it had all gone so wrong.

When they'd first met, they hadn't been able to keep their hands off each other. He and Carly had burned white-hot and then flamed out. He knew all the facts of how and why it had happened, and he'd certainly understood his own heartbreak. He'd seen hers, but he'd never been able to relieve it, to help her. What he'd told his dad was true. Carly may have forgiven him, but she would never forget what they'd been through.

He was getting maudlin. Shaking it off, he finished his job, put away his tools and decided to go tell Carly the job was done.

He drove the long way around to her place, where he saw that her pickup was gone. He was heading back to his own truck when she pulled in and drove straight up to the shed.

"Hi, Luke," she called out as she jumped out of the truck. He was happy to see she hadn't greeted him with her frequent hesitation, but he realized it was because she wasn't focused on him. She hurried to the truck bed and began untying the cords holding down a tarped load.

Still, it was the friendliest greeting he'd received from her so he strolled over to see what she had. He let his appreciative gaze take in the way she looked in her usual jeans, this time paired with a sleeveless blue tank top she wore in spite of the cool temperature. Funny, he'd never realized how much he liked muscles on a woman, even though he'd been trained by his mother and grandmother to respect strength and stamina.

When she joyfully pulled back the cover, he said, "For some reason, I thought this would be a load of plants or gardening equipment, but I'm guessing it's—"

"Brush and bulky," she finished for him, her eyes shining. "Or at least bulky. You want to help me?"

In one easy move, she jumped into the back and began handing down a piano bench with a loose leg, followed by two badly worn and scratched chairs. Excitedly, she said, "Those chairs are mahogany. I can fix them up better than ever. And look at this table. It's maple and it's from the 1950s. It only needs to be cleaned and polished. I'm going to see if Becky Hall wants it. She's been pretty happy with the dinette set she bought from me. And these *lamps*," she declared, holding up two ugly wrought-iron specimens. "They just need to be rewired, but don't they just scream 1970s?"

"I think they scream 'torture chamber,'" he said, taking them and setting them on the ground.

"And there's a matching candelabra." She turned it so he could see the curlicued monstrosity. "It only needs cleaning."

"Or melting down into fishing weights."

She gave him an exasperated look. "I don't think you appreciate vintage furniture, or accessories."

"So it seems."

"A lot of people don't. Every time the county has pickup and I go out looking for items to up-cycle, I'm amazed by the things people no longer value, ones they paid good money for at some time in the past." She pointed to the assortment of treasures she'd found. "Those mahogany chairs, for example. Their craftsmanship is excellent. Just look at the carving on the back. Nobody does that kind of work anymore, except a few artisans. Stripping and refinishing them is going to take some time, but they'll be worth the effort. And, like I said, it's the same every time."

Luke watched her face, the happiness in

her eyes and the way her cheeks turned pink with effort and excitement. He couldn't resist teasing her a little. "Have you considered just going door-to-door and asking for junk?"

She shrugged. "What would be the fun in that? Well, you don't have to appreciate it to help me move it. Come on."

When he saw that she was going to hop down, he held out his hand. She paused for a second before taking it, as if she didn't know exactly what to do. Finally she grasped it and jumped.

When her feet hit the ground, a tremor shook them. She stumbled and grabbed for the side of the truck while Luke tried to steady her. The tremor faded in a couple of seconds.

"Another earthquake," she said, pushing away from the truck. "You know this will never stop as long as the disposal of fracking wastewater continues, not just here, but all over the state."

"I know, Carly."

"Is this what we have to look forward to forever?" She pointed to the rise where the drilling rig was almost completed, looming over her land.

"I wish I had an answer."

She wasn't satisfied with that, if her tight-lipped expression was any indication. He wasn't, either. After a moment he said, "Let's get this finished." She nodded.

Together, they carried her finds into the shed, where she carefully arranged them on the long tables built into one wall. Her tools and supplies for refurbishing were neatly organized, ready for use.

"How long will it take you to get this lot ready for sale?"

She frowned as she glanced up and down the tables. "Probably a month. I've always worked on this kind of thing in the evenings, but now that I've got Dustin, and he's in school, I'm not sure what kind of time I'll have."

The words fell out of his mouth before he even knew they were coming. "I can come over in the evenings, play checkers with him, maybe teach him chess, help him with his homework. He'll probably have a lot to catch up on."

Her eyes widened. "I...I don't know, Luke. That would take up a lot of your time."

He shrugged. "I did say I'd help."

Carly made a scoffing noise. "Let's face it, neither of us knows anything about raising a kid like Dustin."

"No, and I think that was pretty obvious on Saturday. Still can't believe how he changed those signs," Luke agreed.

"I'm glad you stopped Jay from throttling him. I made Dustin burn those signs and make new, G-rated ones."

Luke chuckled. "I guess it's easier, especially with a kid like Dustin, if you start out with them as a baby so you don't have to play catch-up on their behaviors."

"I suppose so. I guess I wouldn't know." Carly looked down, tucked her hands into her back pockets and kicked at the dirt.

"Carly?" Luke waited for her to meet his gaze. "I know you decided to take Dustin on because you felt guilty that you hadn't looked after Era, but did you do it, partly at least, because he's the age our son would have been? Even has black hair and dark eyes like you?"

She shrugged. "Maybe, partly, but he

needs a home, stability, especially now that his mother doesn't want him. He's a good kid, really. You should see him with Era. He's very sweet."

"So, he's got that going for him, at least. Anyway, like I said, I'll come over in the evenings and keep him...positively engaged so you can work out here."

Carly turned away, hunching her shoulders for a moment before she straightened her back, squared her shoulders and said, "I appreciate everything you've done to help me with him, but I don't think it's a good idea for you to be here every evening..."

"My dad spooked you, didn't he?"

Her lips drew into a grim line. "I was surprised to see him, that's all."

"*I* was surprised he came into your shop, but I knew he'd be around at some point. He can't let go of any project, even one he's told me is all mine."

Carly rubbed the back of her hand across her forehead, leaving a streak of dirt behind. "I clearly recall he was very controlling."

Luke pulled down his jacket sleeve to cover the heel of his hand and used it to wipe off the dirt. "I promise I'll keep him away from you." *This time*, he added silently.

She nodded. "Thank you."

"Carly, I never really knew what he said to you before you left. I assumed it was the same thing he said to me, that I needed to marry someone who could do my career some good. That was never what I wanted, and he was just mad because we'd gotten married without telling him."

"He always seemed to be mad, at least at me." Carly shook her head. "No. I never really said what he told me, but it was pretty much the same thing, and it doesn't matter now. At the time, you and I weren't talking much. Then Gemma and Lisa came to see me, and I realized I wanted to go home, be with my parents. Gemma told me later, after she became a midwife, that my desire to get away was normal, that I had severe postpartum depression." She looked up. "I came home because I needed to heal. I'd just lost a baby."

"I know. I'd lost one, too."

"True knot," Carly said in a tone so low he could barely hear her. "Did you know that's what it was called?"

Her throat was working as if the words were fighting to come out. His gut clenched and he fought down the sickness that rose in his throat. "Yes. I know. I did research on it...afterward. The baby twisted and turned so much in the womb that he tied a knot..."

"In the c-cord." The word lurched from her. "He...never had a chance, but he moved so much, was so active... Do you think I could have stopped him? Calmed him down somehow?"

She looked at him with naked sorrow drenching her eyes. Her bottom lip trembled. The expression on her face was such an echo of the pain he'd caused her, his conscience kicked at him.

"I've seen other women do that—put their hands on their bellies and rub or pat their babies until they settle down. I tried that, but it didn't work very well. He...he was always so active."

"Oh, Carly, it wasn't your fault," he said, wishing he could take this pain from her, and from himself, to be finished with how sorry he was, how guilty he felt. But it was always with him, and now he knew it was always with her. Tenderly, he cradled her chin and closed the gap between them, covering her mouth with his.

He absorbed her soft gasp of surprise, then reveled in her warm response as she pressed her lips to his and lifted her hand to the back of his neck. Before he could put his arms around her, though, she pulled away, lowering her head, stepping back. "We…we can't, Luke."

"I'm sorry, Carly. I didn't…plan that."

She cleared her throat. "It's okay," she said, looking up. Her lips still trembled but she tried to smile. "At least you shaved this morning. It wasn't like kissing a toothbrush."

He laughed and the awkward moment passed. But the rattling storm of feelings remained.

PRESCHOOL MATH, DUSTIN THOUGHT, his disgust growing. He'd learned this stuff a year ago— more than a year ago—when one school, he couldn't remember the name of it, had put him in beginning algebra as soon as that particular foster mom had enrolled him and he'd been tested. He wished they'd test him again.

He liked the look of shock on their faces when he didn't turn out to be stupid.

Stupid was what his new best enemy, Brando Poster, thought he was. Brando. What a dumb name. Where did that come from? Did his mom just chop the *n* off *Brandon* so her kid would sound cool?

The big kid with the mean eyes was anything but cool.

They'd been in three classes together today, and he knew the guy was going to grab him as soon as class was over. Brando had tried to get close enough to bully him at lunch, but the aide had spotted him and moved in so Brando couldn't make a move. Dustin figured she'd seen how the guy worked.

Brando didn't know he'd already spied a way out. When he'd been in the office this morning, the principal's door was open and he'd seen another door beyond that one—a door he was sure would lead outside. He would use it. He could get past the secretary. Dismissal at any school was too busy for her to keep an eye on everyone who came into the office. If the door had an alarm on it, he'd run and if they caught him, he'd say sorry, that he got lost and was scared by the alarm.

Of course, he'd have to watch out for the principal. He'd seen a lot of principals. They almost always were out of their offices at dismissal time, watching the kids, teachers, parents. Whether it was the principal or Brando, Dustin didn't think he'd have any trouble getting away. He was smaller and quicker. He was supposed to meet Carly a couple of blocks away so she could take him to the hospital to see his grandma. Carly didn't want to get stuck in the traffic jam at the parent pickup area so she had showed him where to meet her. He planned to be there.

As soon as the bell rang, he was out the door, but he hadn't counted on his unfamiliarity with the hallways, and the increased traffic of kids, slowing him down. Apparently some of the high schoolers exited through the middle school. The sudden influx of kids meant he could barely move.

He got caught up in the crush and was pushed backward to where he'd started. Struggling to move, he made a wrong turn and came face-to-face with the one he was trying to avoid.

Brando grinned as he stepped out from the gap between two banks of lockers. He reached out, quicker than Dustin expected, and grabbed the front of his new shirt.

"Hey, new boy, where you goin'?" he asked, tightening his fist.

"None of your business. Let go of me and get outta my way." Dustin tried to back up while peeling Brando's fingers off his shirt, but there was a solid stream of bodies behind him. He couldn't move or join the departing crowd with Brando holding him.

The bigger boy pulled him closer. "Uh-uh. We don't like new guys around here." He lifted his hand and made a fist. Dustin tried to duck away but felt himself pressed up against someone who placed a hand on his shoulder.

Before Dustin could even begin to deal with this new threat, Jay Morton said, "I don't know what you think you're doing, Brando, but it'd better stop. Let go of him."

Brando looked up and his eyes widened as his hand opened. Dustin jerked back, trying to get away from Jay, even as he wished he could see what Brando was seeing. Brando was big, but Jay was a lot bigger.

"You picking on the new kid?"

Brando's mouth turned down as he tried to look innocent. "Nah, Jay. Not me. I was just…saying hi."

"I don't think you were. I think you're picking on the new kid, and I think it better stop."

"Uh, yeah, Jay. Sure. I didn't know he was a friend of yours."

Jay didn't answer. Brando scooted past them and fled.

Dustin couldn't believe Jay had stood up for him. He whipped around to face him, but the older boy was already walking away. Didn't even look back.

The anger Dustin had felt all day made a weird shift in his chest. After what he'd done to Jay, he'd expected revenge. He'd never thought Jay would actually have his back. Why'd he do that?

The question only added to the mix of confusion he felt. He wanted to lash out, but he didn't know who to swing at. He frowned. Maybe he'd wanted to get into a fight with

Brando to release some of his angry energy. Jay had robbed him of that chance, but also probably saved him from a beating.

Head down, he finally found the exit that took him to the street he would follow for two blocks to meet Carly. He'd go see his grandma. She was the only person in his life who didn't confuse him.

CHAPTER THIRTEEN

THE LOW HUM and rhythmic thumping began on a windless afternoon a few days after Upcycle's grand opening. Carly, accustomed to quiet, or the occasional passing of a car, straightened from picking the last of the pole beans. It took her a moment to realize what the noise was.

"They're drilling," she said aloud, whirling around to look at the rig. She'd known it would happen, but she hadn't expected it so soon. Looking at the ground under her boots, she imagined the drill going down, cracking through the earth. She wished she could imagine the future as easily, to know what to expect.

Dismayed, and feeling helpless to protect her land, she loaded the beans into the truck and headed into town to stop by Upcycle, make deliveries and pick up Dustin for his visit with his grandmother. Dustin had insisted he was starving, so they'd stopped for hamburgers and didn't arrive home until after dark.

As they stepped from the truck, Carly sniffed the air, recognizing the heavy stench of diesel fuel. Of course, she thought. Since the extraction plant was at a higher elevation, the fumes from the engines would drift over her property on a windless day and settle into the low places. She hadn't considered that. How many more unpleasant surprises were headed her way? Maybe if she kept the windows closed, it wouldn't be too bad inside the house.

Carly looked at Dustin's heavy backpack and said, "I'm guessing you've got homework?"

Dustin nodded but before he could answer, he started coughing. When he could speak again, he said, "It smells like the place where my dad used to work."

"You mean the oil field?"

"Yes." He started into the house, but they both turned when they heard a truck approaching. It was Luke, who greeted them with a wave and joined them on the porch.

"I came to see if you're ready for a game of chess," he said. "But it looks like you just got home."

"Yeah," Dustin said. "And I've got home… home—" His eyes began to water and his nostrils flared as he gulped a wheezing breath and went into another coughing spasm.

Carly took his backpack from his shoulders as Luke supported him until he could take another struggling breath.

"Dustin, do you have asthma?" Carly asked.

He nodded. "But not…in a long time."

"Do you have an inhaler?"

He shook his head and wheezed again, fighting for breath.

"Come on," Luke said, scooping Dustin up. "We're going to the emergency room. Thank God, the hospital is finally open."

He rushed to the truck with Carly running ahead to open the door and buckle the limp boy into the seat. She climbed in beside him and held him upright while Luke jumped in behind the wheel and broke the speed limit getting him to the emergency room.

Nathan Smith was on duty and, after examining Dustin, he administered an epinephrine shot. When he saw that it was making Dustin's breathing easier, he signaled for Carly and Luke to follow him into the hallway.

"Do you have any idea what triggered this attack?" he asked. "Any change in atmosphere, exposure to an allergen?"

"No. I don't know." Carly shook her head and tears filled her eyes. "I didn't even know he *had* asthma. What kind of mother doesn't know her kid has asthma?"

"Don't beat yourself up, Carly," Luke said. "You're new at this."

She didn't need the reminder and she wiped tears from her eyes as she tried to think. "When we got home, the diesel fumes were hanging over the place. He said it smelled like the oil field where his dad used to work."

Nathan frowned. "Diesel?"

"We're testing out the engines that will drive the drill," Luke said.

"That's probably it. I'll prescribe an inhaler for him. We'll show you how to use it as soon as he feels his throat or chest begin to tighten. You can take him home tonight but you might want to keep him home from school tomorrow." Nathan turned away. "I've got to check on another patient. I'll be back."

Carly turned on Luke and spoke in low tones. "Diesel fumes? He was a perfectly healthy boy until tonight. How am I going to keep him well if he's breathing diesel fumes every day?"

"When there's wind, it won't be so bad."

"No, they'll blow onto some other lucky family's land."

Luke's face tightened. "Carly, I—"

"You what?" she asked, throwing her hands wide. "You can't tell me what's going on, you can't give me a heads-up or any kind of warning that you're going to be poisoning the air?"

"I'll fix this," Luke insisted, taking out his cell phone. "I'll tell the crew to shut down the engines for tonight—"

"So they can start bright and early in the morning." Angry and frustrated, she stepped away, ready to return to Dustin.

Luke started walking in the other direction. "I said I'll fix this. Let me know when you're ready to go home."

"I don't want any help from you. I'll call

Gemma to take us home." Her hand sliced the air. "Just stay away from us so I can... figure this out."

Carly could hear him stalking away as she returned to Dustin, who was breathing more easily but was restless, ready to go home. She called Gemma, who took them back to the house, checked to make sure they knew how to use his new inhaler, then returned to her own home.

A breeze had kicked up, clearing the air, and Carly could no longer hear the engines, but she double-checked the window in Dustin's room to make sure it was tightly shut. He was twisting in his bed, shoving off the covers then pulling them up again. Gemma had warned her that the epinephrine shot would stimulate him, make it hard for him to sleep.

"I'm glad that stink is gone," he said, turning on his side. "The whole place where we lived smelled like that. We moved after Dad..."

"Do you remember how old you were when you had your first asthma attack?" Cautiously, Carly picked up the desk chair and set it beside the bed. The light from the hallway sent a warm slash of brightness into the room.

"Nah. I was just a little kid." He yawned. "Mom and Dad would fight sometimes, 'specially if Mom was gone when Dad got home. Mom liked to go out."

Shocked, she stared at him. "You mean, she left you alone?"

Dustin yawned again. "Yeah, but it was okay. I watched TV or played video games until Dad got home."

"How old were you?"

"Six, seven, eight. I was eight when Dad got killed." His eyes drifted shut. "I hate that smell," he murmured as he drifted off to sleep.

Carly leaned forward and dropped her face into her palms, letting the tears flow but stifling any sobs that might wake him once again.

Poor Joey Salyer had picked a real winner for a wife, she thought, a woman who would leave a small child with asthma alone at home so she could go out partying. Era must have known and that would have added to her reasons not to tell the authorities that Dustin was with her.

Carly had to protect him, but she felt helpless. The effects of Luke's extraction site were out of her hands. Wiping her eyes, she stood, replaced the chair and headed for bed. There had to be a way.

LUKE KNEW HE was the last person Carly would want to see, but he pulled into her driveway the next morning anyway. It had been like a knife through the heart to see Dustin struggling for breath. Knowing he was responsible made it even worse. Hurting Carly, yet again, was the last thing he had intended. He doubted he could make her see that, but he had to try.

As soon as he stopped his truck, she emerged from one of the greenhouses, fists clenched, arms pumping as she strode toward him.

"I'm going to find an attorney who will help me stop you," she said. "This can't go on and I'm not going to risk Dustin's health."

"The diesel engines are gone," he said,

holding up his hands. "I'm replacing them with natural gas ones so there's less risk."

"But there's still risk, right?"

"Very little." When she made a sound of disgust and looked away, he said, "I'm sorry. We didn't consider any other type of engine, just went with what looked to be the most cost-efficient at the time."

"I think there are many things you didn't consider."

"I never intended to harm Dustin or you." He stopped and took a deep breath. "How is he today?"

She looked as if she didn't want to answer but she finally said, "Better. He insisted on going to school."

"Quite a change from last week."

"He likes showing off how smart he is." Her lips quirked. "In spite of all he's been through, he does focus on school. Era said she talked to him about how important it is to get an education."

An awkward silence stretched between them until Carly gave him a questioning glance and asked, "How much is it costing you?"

"What?"

"Switching over to natural gas engines."

"More than I want to think about." In fact, it had pushed the project way over budget and thrown off their timeline. And they didn't even know if Shelby's process would work or not.

She cleared her throat. "Thank you for doing that for Dustin."

Luke nodded. It hadn't only been for Dustin. "Okay if I come back and play chess with him this evening?"

She pressed her lips together and didn't reply.

"I know I might not be the ideal male role model," he said, watching her face. "But I'm what's available, and the kid doesn't have a dad."

Her gaze bounced up to his and her face spasmed as if in regret. "Okay. He should be finished with his homework and ready for chess by seven."

Puzzled over the way she had looked at him, Luke nodded and returned to his truck, grateful she'd given him another chance.

WHEN LUKE CAME back that evening to play a game of chess with Dustin, Carly fled to her work shed. She examined the two mahogany chairs under bright light, unable to quite decide the source of the surface scratches. These two looked like they'd been caught in a tornado, which, in Oklahoma, was a distinct possibility. She would strip and sand them and then apply a rich varnish to finish, which antiques dealers would frown on. She wasn't an antiques dealer, though, and up-cycling meant the item would be improved when she completed it.

The next piece she examined was the piano bench, and she discovered that the leg could be easily repaired. She didn't understand why people didn't make the effort to perform such an easy fix. This had been at the end of Mrs. Held's driveway. The sheriff's mother was quite elderly and probably hadn't felt like dealing with the broken leg. Staring at it for a few seconds, Carly realized it was the bench to her grand piano, which she still played when she felt strong enough.

Carly shook her head. She didn't know how the bench had ended up on the trash heap, but she would repair it and return it to Mrs.

Held, who even now was probably wondering where it had gone.

As she worked her way down the table, assessing and planning, making notes and checking supplies, she couldn't keep her mind off Luke and what he'd done for Dustin. He'd caught her by surprise with his announcement that he was switching out the engines. What had Robert said about the added expense? She could only imagine.

She'd been furious over the diesel fumes, but Luke had made amends. Also, when he'd walked through the door this evening, Dustin had been glad to see him, eager to play checkers, which his father had taught him. Maybe the two of them would develop a friendship. Dustin needed a responsible male friend.

And what about her? What did she need? Carly sat on a stool by her worktable and thought about the way Luke had kissed her.

Thinking about it made her want to weep with longing, frustration and regret. Seeing him again, spending so much time with him, made her remember what it had been like to be crazy in love with him and then to lose everything. Over the years she'd tried to sort through it and had realized they'd started their marriage on a shaky foundation of attraction and then they'd lost their child.

They had talked about him at last, standing out there in her yard, surrounded by gardening implements, pieces of broken furniture and the tools she used to rebuild those broken pieces. Really, they were the tools she'd used to rebuild her life. She was shaken to realize he didn't blame her for the baby's death. Since she had been so broken after the miscarriage, prostrate with grief and unable to talk about it, she'd thought he blamed her as much as she blamed herself. It was a relief to know he didn't and it gave her the first stirrings of a new peace she hadn't known.

She felt shaky, noodle-kneed, as she always did after being in a boat. It would take her a while to come to grips with this. For all the hard work she'd done to make her businesses successful, she'd done most of it to keep herself occupied and too tired to think about her loss. In fact, she had a mental picture of her heart with a no-admittance sign on it.

But Luke was right. She'd taken responsibility for Dustin partly because she'd let Era down and partly because she thought her son would have looked like him. Mostly, though, it was because he'd been so vulnerable in spite of his toughness. After what he'd told her last night, she knew he needed someone on his side even if he fought it.

She placed both hands on the worktable and bent her head forward as her thoughts sorted themselves out. Somehow, seeing Luke again, receiving Wendolin's trunk and all the family items in it, had helped spark her need for a child. Not to replace the one she'd lost, because that would never be possible, especially after all this time, but because she knew she could take care of one. All these years, her heart had ached for a child of her own. She had buried that need in hard work, but it had never gone away.

She only had to remember not to depend on Luke. He probably wouldn't be around after the six months were up. The project would be done and he would move on. She needed to be okay with that.

As if to emphasize that point, the table beneath her hands trembled and the shop lights swayed.

"Another earthquake," she said aloud, looking up. It stopped as quickly as it had begun.

The short duration didn't make it any less worrisome. There were more and more of them all the time, often of higher magnitude. She still wanted to know if Dr. Wayne's process would increase the problem, or contaminate her water, but she couldn't get an answer.

She had kissed Luke. She had talked to him about the baby, lost her composure, been comforted by him and kissed him. She hadn't expected it, hadn't wanted it, and the kiss had agitated feelings she'd kept under control for years.

Getting involved with Luke, falling in love with him again, couldn't happen. True, she was older, more mature, independent and modestly successful—in fact, everything she hadn't been at nineteen. But that didn't mean she could handle another broken heart.

DUSTIN WON ANOTHER game of chess.

"I can't believe I keep losing to a twelve-year-old," Luke grumbled, causing Dustin to grin. "Are you sure you've never played before?"

"Maybe. A little," the boy admitted. "My dad showed me when I was eight, then one of my mom's boyfriends played with me until he knew he didn't have to be nice to me for my mom to like him. She liked all those guys that came around after Dad died."

Luke's gaze bounced from the chessboard to Dustin's face. His expression was completely neutral as he looked at the game. He was merely reporting what had happened, as if it didn't affect him at all. Dustin must have learned at a young age to hide his emotions as much as possible because that's how people hurt you.

The sorrow Luke felt for this boy twisted his gut.

Since he had lost his own mother when he was only nineteen, Luke knew a little of what Dustin felt. And losing his child to a one-in-a-million miscarriage had created a deep-rooted grief he'd never get over, even though he'd learned to live with it.

And Carly felt that same grief, carried it with her every day. Strangely, he felt grateful that her sorrow was as deep as his own. It made carrying that burden a little easier.

"Hey, Luke," Dustin complained. "It's no fun playing with a guy who lets me win."

Luke blinked and looked at the board. How many games had he lost now? "Oh, yeah?" he said, meeting Dustin's eyes. "Well, get ready, buddy, because you're going down."

Dustin rolled his eyes and reset the board.

To CARLY'S RELIEF Dustin seemed to settle into school within a few days. Or at least, she'd thought so until she received a call from the vice principal. Chet Franklin had been her eleventh-grade government and history teacher.

"You've got a live one here, Carly."

"What do you mean?" She immediately had visions of behavior issues and school suspensions. Afraid this was going to be a difficult conversation, she cut the motor on the four-wheeler and sat, staring at her pumpkin field.

Mr. Franklin cleared his throat. "He's smart. I mean scary smart."

"Really?" Pride filled her heart as she grinned. She glanced around the gardens, wishing there was someone to share this with.

"I have to admit that I thought he was, but I'm not an educator, so I wasn't sure."

"Well, now you can be sure. Even though he's bounced from school to school, he's far above grade level in every subject, especially math."

"Well, that's wonderful, isn't it?"

"It is, as long as we can keep him challenged. What would you think of putting him in a high school algebra class?"

"You're kidding! He's that smart?"

"Absolutely."

"I don't know." She thought for a long moment. "Are you sure he could handle it? I knew he was smart, but that sounds like genius level."

"Not quite, but certainly superintelligent. I think he's used to hiding how bright he is."

Carly thought about the conflicts between Dustin and Jay. She wondered now if Dustin had pulled those tricks on Jay because he was desperate to show how smart he was as well as to test the limits to see how far he could go.

Still, she hesitated. "He's not a big kid, and he would be in with all those almost grown-ups."

"I think he can handle it. Think about it and let me know. If it's acceptable to you, he can start next week. The teacher is all for it. He'd love to see how having a twelve-year-old in that class will shake things up."

"I guarantee he'll shake things up," she said with a sigh. "I'll think about this, Mr. Franklin." She would certainly talk it over with Dustin and Era, and maybe Luke. Dustin's education was a nice, neutral subject.

"Also, Carly, there's something else. I've already talked to Dustin about it, but could you please ask him to quit drawing caricatures of the other kids in his classes? And the teachers?"

"Caricatures," she said faintly, recalling Jay's face drawn on pumpkins.

"They're not mean. In fact, they're flattering. He drew one of me that gave me a full head of hair, took off forty pounds and put me in a captain's uniform at the wheel of an ocean liner. I'm getting it framed."

Carly chuckled. "I hear a 'but' coming."

"They're papering the school."

"He's not selling them, is he?"

"Not yet."

"I'll talk to him."

When she took Dustin to the hospital that afternoon, they were happy to see that Era was well enough to be moved to the extended care facility attached to the hospital, where she would receive daily physical and occupational therapy. Era was regaining her strength and her health, as well as her interest in the world. She wanted to return to her normal activities as soon as possible.

After their visit, Dustin scooted into the truck and snapped his seat belt into place. "When she's better, we're going home,"

"That might not be for a while, Dustin." Carly pulled out of the parking lot even as she glanced at his face, trying to gauge his mood and decide how much to say.

"I can take care of her. I did it before. If she doesn't get sick again, I can take care of her," he said with utter confidence. "The hospital in Reston is open now, so if she gets sick again, she can go there. That guy, Dr. Smith, can be her doctor. I just need to learn how to cook," he added.

"It's not that simple, Dustin," Carly said, but he wasn't listening.

"Dustin, your grandma isn't going to want you to give up your own life, your interests, your social life to take care of her."

"But I can do it. I can stay and take care of her." He was adamant, so Carly let it drop for now. Era was still many weeks from independence, anyway.

Although no one had told him, Dustin seemed to understand that his mother wasn't coming for him. He never asked about her, or about having to return to Waco. With that threat gone, he likely saw no reason he couldn't live with Era.

Carly wanted to let him continue in his fantasy for a while longer. He had a stable life and was doing well in school.

She decided that since Dustin seemed fairly happy today she would talk about the caricatures.

"I got a call from Mr. Franklin today, the vice principal at the middle school."

Dustin looked out the window and shook his head. "Sheesh. I've only been there a week."

"You're not really in trouble," she said quickly. "But he says your drawings are taking over the school."

"Kids like 'em."

"I'm sure they do, and you're a talented artist, but Mr. Franklin says they're distracting and you're using too much paper, even though they're very good." She paused. "By the way, where do you get the paper?"

"Off the classroom printers."

"Oh, that must be popular with the teachers," she said dryly.

"Nah, they don't like it."

"You have to stop that. I'm sure school budgets are tight enough without you using up reams of printer paper."

"If I bring my own paper, can I keep doing them? Kids like 'em," he repeated.

Carly frowned and then looked at him. "That's how you're making friends, isn't it?"

Dustin shrugged.

Carly knew he had an odd unwillingness to admit he really enjoyed anything. Maybe he was afraid it would be taken away from him.

"I'll think about it," she said.

"Sheesh," he muttered again, looking out the window at the passing scenery.

"We can come up with a solution, Dustin, but it would be better if we both worked on it."

When he didn't answer, she went on. "I admit I don't know anything about having to move from school to school, place to place, but you're here now and this is where you'll stay. This is your hometown now. It's also your grandma's hometown. She's respected in the community."

His uneasy look told her he was listening. "Yeah, so?"

"So you want to be someone who makes her proud, not someone who breaks the rules."

She let him think about that as they drove in silence for a few miles. "There's something else, too. Mr. Franklin says he and your math teacher want to put you in the algebra class at the high school."

"Huh?" His face screwed up in question.

"It's true. They think you need more of a challenge."

Dustin crossed his arms over his chest and sat back. "They just want to make it hard for me, make me fail. *You* want me to fail."

Carly gritted her teeth. "*Nobody* wants that."

His assumption hurt, but she knew it was only a knee-jerk reaction. In spite of his attitude, her heart warmed to him. Given all that had happened to him, he still wasn't defeated by life. She could relate to that.

"Is your math class too easy?"

"It's baby math."

"Well, then, I'd think you'd want the challenge. You can at least try it."

He was silent all the way home, but when they stepped from the truck, he said, "Do you think my grandma would like it if I took the algebra class?"

"You can ask her, but I think she would be proud of you. Everyone wants to be proud of their kids and grandkids."

Dustin gave her another of those suspicious looks, but he finally said, "Okay. I'll try it, but if it's too hard, I can go back to the one I'm in now, right?"

"Right." Carly gave him a one-armed hug, but he ducked away. Still, she saw a flicker of a smile on his lips.

DUSTIN HOVERED IN the doorway, his gaze jerking around the classroom of high school kids, looking for a place to sit. Of course, the first person he saw was Jay Morton, though he sat near the back of the room. Jay crossed his arms over his chest and stared at him as if he was daring Dustin to come near.

Of all the junked-up messes, Dustin thought and he tried to turn away, back into the hallway, but Mr. Franklin was right behind him.

"It's okay, Dustin. Go on in. This is the right classroom."

That's what you think, mister. The kids were shuffling, looking at him, questioning how this shrimp had landed there with all these sharks, although they'd been told he was coming. Maybe they'd thought it was a joke—a seventh-grader, and a new one at that, enrolling in their algebra class.

While this commotion was going on, the vice principal went to talk to the teacher, Mr. Gilpin, who smiled and nodded at Dustin. They'd met the day before and Mr. G, as he liked to be called, had explained how things worked in his class—although he hadn't said anything about how the other kids would react.

That left Dustin to find his own seat.

Standing in the middle of one row, he met Jay's eyes. Reluctantly, Jay motioned for Dustin to come closer and pointed to the seat next to him. Dustin hesitated but took the seat just so he could get out of everyone's line of sight.

Jay leaned over and whispered, "*Don't* embarrass me."

Dustin didn't respond. What did the big jerk think he was going to do to embarrass him? Turning to face the front, he was soon captivated by the interactive electronic screen with the day's lesson laid out step-by-step.

Even though they'd been in this class for weeks, some of the students seemed to be confused by the new concept they were learning, although Mr. G explained, gave examples, worked through it with them on the screen, then explained again.

Dustin could see every step so clearly that excitement rushed through him. He could do this. For the first time in months he felt he was where he needed to be. Mr. G asked a question to check for understanding and Dustin's hand shot up. When he answered correctly, Mr. G praised him and a deadly silence fell over the rest of the room, followed by murmuring and shuffling. Confused, he looked around. How come no one else got it?

Jay glared at him and Dustin realized no one else got the correct answer because no one else understood it. They thought he was just showing off, trying to be teacher's pet.

Someone across the room made a sound of disgust and the boy behind him made kissing noises.

Dustin sat quietly through the remainder of the class. Even though he loved this math, he didn't belong there.

He didn't belong anywhere.

ERA SALYER'S FACE shone with happiness as she told Carly and Dustin her good news. "I never thought I could get that much for my land—too rocky for farming, or much of anything except raising chickens—but this man just showed up and said he wants to expand his gravel digging operation. The highway department pays good money for gravel for road maintenance and he's got a contract with them."

"Be sure to hang on to your mineral rights," Carly said, thinking of the hard lesson she'd learned.

"I can't imagine I would need them. There's no oil or gas on my land."

"You never know."

Era wasn't really listening. "This is an answer to my prayers," she said, giving them a dazed smile. "I can't believe it was so easy to find a buyer, especially since I wasn't even looking for one."

Dustin looked from one woman to the other, his distress growing. "But, Grandma, if you sell your house, where will we live?"

"Oh," she said in dismay. "I didn't think." She looked at Dustin and shook her head helplessly. "I...I guess I could buy a house here in town, what with the money from the sale of my land, but I wanted to put that in a college fund for you, Dustin." Her eyes were full of tears as she spoke to Carly. "He's really smart, you know."

"I've discovered that."

"I don't know what to do. I don't really want the responsibility of another house, and they've got an apartment for me at Sooner Community."

"That would be the perfect place for you, with the other retirees," Carly reassured her even as her gaze stayed fixed on Dustin's face. "There are always activities going on there and it's right in Reston."

Dustin shook his head helplessly, his anxious eyes fixed on Era's face. "But I can live there, too, right? With you?"

"You can visit," Era said, sitting forward and reaching for his hand. "Every day, just like you do now." Seeing the consternation on her grandson's face, tears started into her eyes. "I...I can't take care of you, Dustin. I proved that when I was trying to hide you and I made a mess of everything."

"You were trying to do what you thought was best for him, Era," Carly reassured her.

Sunk in distress, Era wasn't listening. She grabbed a tissue and mopped at her eyes. "I made a mess of things, of everything. I didn't know what to do. I didn't have enough food for you, Dusty. I was afraid they'd take you and I'd never see you again, ever. Then I got sick..."

His eyes were full of terror as he asked, "Will I have to go back to foster care...or to my mom?"

"No, no, honey," Era sobbed. "She doesn't want you back."

"Era!" Carly gasped.

Dustin's face was stiff with shock. "What? What do you mean, Grandma? Did my mom say that?"

"Oh, no." Era breathed the words as horrified realization settled over her. "I didn't mean to tell you that, honey, but I'm afraid it's true. After you ran away, she said she couldn't handle you and for the state of Texas to take you if they could find you."

Dustin's mouth was working and his chin trembled. "She gave me away? Like…like a puppy? I have to go back to Texas? To foster care? But…but your house is home. Where… where I belong."

"It's going to be okay, honey," Era sobbed.

"Not if I have to go away, go live someplace else *again*." He stared at his grandmother, the only person in his life he'd thought he could trust.

Carly jumped to her feet. "But that's not going to happen, Dustin. You're staying with me."

She hurried around the bed, reaching out to him, but he spun away from her and lunged out the door. In the hallway, a cart crashed against a wall and someone shouted for him to be careful.

CHAPTER FOURTEEN

"DUSTIN, STOP."

Carly rushed after him, hoping the security door would stop him, but someone had just entered and the door hadn't closed all the way, leaving enough space for a skinny kid to slip out once he'd dropped his backpack.

The receptionist punched in the code to re-open the door, but the fifteen-second delay meant that Dustin was long gone by the time she reached the front sidewalk. At a run, she circled the entire building, looking up and down the streets.

"Oh, Dustin," she whispered. "Where will you go?" She already knew he was very clever and could make his way in the woods without being detected.

Toncaville was twenty-five miles from Reston. He would probably hitchhike, as she suspected he had done from Waco. Even after reaching Reston, though, it was a long walk to his grandmother's old place, but if he was determined enough, he could do it.

The house was locked up. She didn't know if he had a key, but the water and electricity were shut off, too. It made her heart clench to think of him alone, hungry, scared, in that cold, abandoned house, and feeling like the whole world had turned its back on him.

She hurried inside, scooped up his backpack and went to reassure a tearful Era that she would find Dustin and let her know he was safe. Then she called Lisa, asking for help.

"Are you going to call the sheriff?"

"Not yet. Dustin is terrified of law enforcement, thinks they're going to slap him in jail. And I know it's dangerous for him to hitchhike, so we'll have to pray someone trustworthy picks him up."

"You'll need more help, Carly. Better call Luke," Lisa advised. "I'll get hold of Gemma and anyone else I can find, and start looking. If he's hitchhiking, it will take him a while to get here, so we'll have time to organize."

Carly called Luke and then phoned Jay to let him know what was going on and that she wouldn't be home for a while. She hurried to her truck and started searching the streets closest to the hospital, looking for an angry, dark-haired boy who'd just had his heart broken.

JAY SLIPPED HIS cell phone into his pocket and kicked a tire on the four-wheeler. Hadn't that little punk caused enough trouble today? This whole month in fact? All summer? It was like there wasn't any end to the problems he could cause.

Jay went back to work for the next half hour, but the more he thought about Dustin, the madder he got.

Sheena drove up and he told her what was going on. "Can you finish here?" he asked as she stepped out of her vehicle. "I'm going to help look for the little creeper."

She planted her hands on her hips and shook her head at him. "You know, it might help if you quit thinking of him as a creeper. Do you call him that to his face?"

"Well, yeah. That's what he is."

"He's a messed-up kid," she said. "You don't know what it's like to live like he has.

As soon as Carly told us about him, I knew you were clueless."

"Hey!"

She sighed as she said, "You've had the same mom and dad your whole life, and they take care of you, like my mom takes care of me and my brothers and sisters. My dad does, too, when he remembers we exist. And he's sober."

Jay stuck out his chin, ready to argue, but she shook her head again and held up her hand. "Save your breath. I've got the work of three people to finish. Go ahead and look for him, but be nice to him if you find him."

"Did I tell you what he wrote on the signs down at the stand?" He jabbed his thumb toward the road.

"Six times. Maybe he was mad because you treat him like he's your enemy."

"He is. I don't know why you can't see that."

"You're only mad because you're twice as big as he is and he's twice as smart. *And* he tricked you. Be nice to him." She turned her back and walked away.

"Bossy woman," he muttered.

Jay had to actively look for him this time, not wait for him to stumble into a trap. He wouldn't take his motorcycle. It was too loud and he figured he might have to sneak up on the kid at some point.

He removed a flashlight from the bike's saddlebags and climbed into the four-wheeler. Carly wouldn't mind if he took it to check out the Salyer place. As he started off, he tried to determine how long it would take Dustin to walk from town after hitchhiking from Toncaville, if that's what he'd done.

The kid could have hitchhiked anywhere if he thought nobody wanted him. Guilt kicked at Jay. Maybe Sheena was a little bit right. Maybe he could cut the kid some slack, but he was so annoying. Reminding himself that he was doing this to help Carly, he started trying to think like a desperate kid.

If Jay were making that hike, he would stick to the road, ducking into the underbrush whenever a car approached. But Dustin was probably sneakier than he was. After all, he'd somehow made it from Waco, Texas, to Reston, Oklahoma, without anyone catching him or becoming suspicious of a kid traveling alone. Jay still didn't know how Dustin had done that.

As he drove, Jay tried to turn the time, speed and distance Dustin could travel from town into a math problem, but then he couldn't solve it. Besides, Dustin was a fast runner, so that would change the outcome, anyway.

That was another thing that ticked him off. Dustin was a smokin' math genius. There was no doubt about that. A seventh-grader in a high school algebra class was something you just didn't see every day. Not in their town where everyone knew everyone and kids grew up together, knowing the smartest ones in their grade.

Since he and Dustin knew each other, kids in their class would expect him to be responsible for the kid—or to convince Dustin to let them copy his homework. That wasn't going to happen. Just because Dustin was living with Jay's employer didn't make Jay responsible for him—even if he was beginning to feel a little sorry for him.

He pulled into Mrs. Salyer's rutted driveway and steered the four-wheeler as far into the tall weeds and undergrowth as he could. Then, walking on the outsides of his feet to minimize the sound of his footsteps, he explored all the outbuildings, flicking on his flashlight in short bursts like he'd seen a detective do on television. When he found nothing except chicken coops and abandoned farm equipment, he made his way toward the house. Standing at the corner of the front yard, he could watch both the front and side doors.

Sure enough, as dusk was falling, he saw movement in the shadows and then Dustin made for the side door. Running all out, Jay got to him before he could get it open, grabbed his arm and spun him around.

"Hold it, kid," he said.

"Let go of me!" Dustin yelled, trying to wiggle away.

Jay held on tight. "Why do you have to be such a jerk? Why are you scaring Carly like this? She actually *likes* you and she's worried about you."

"None of your business!" the younger boy yelled back, then called him a string of dirty names.

"Hey! Do you want me to wash your mouth out with soap?"

"You…and…and whose army?" Dustin asked as he twisted and turned, trying to get away. He aimed a kick at Jay's shins, which he managed to avoid.

"Ah, Dustin, don't you realize how good you've got it here?"

To Jay's surprise, Dustin went stiff in his arms then seemed to lose all his strength and fight as he slumped. Jay stumbled and had to put one foot back to steady himself as he held on to the suddenly boneless boy.

"I don't have it good," Dustin said around a sob. "I don't 'cause nobody wants me."

"What are you talking about?"

Haltingly, Dustin reported what he'd learned that day but broke down before he finished.

"Dude," Jay said, making sure Dustin was steady on his feet, then taking another step back to give the boy space to knuckle the tears from his eyes. "That sucks, but Carly wants you."

"No. Nobody does."

"Did Carly *say* she didn't want you?"

"No, but she's trying to be nice."

"She *is* nice. That's why you should stay. She's done a lot for you. If Carly wants to keep you, you should stay. I mean, where else are you gonna go?" He paused, watching to see what effect his words had and remembering what Sheena had said about how his parents took care of him.

"I don't know."

"Your mom doesn't want you to come back?"

"No. She told me she was sorry she had me, especially after my dad died and she couldn't find no one to take care of her, not if she had me. She had money they gave her when my dad died, money from… What do you call it?"

"I don't know. Insurance?"

"Yeah. The oil company he worked for gave her a lot of money, but she hasn't got it now."

"What happened to it?"

"She bought stuff and her boyfriends took it and bought stuff. She doesn't like to work and none of her boyfriends liked me. That's why she put me in foster homes and that's why I ran off."

"Dude," Jay repeated in horror, stretching the word out. His mom got mad at him sometimes, but he knew she loved him and wanted him around. He couldn't even wrap his mind around having his mom say she wished he hadn't been born.

"But that's her problem, not yours. Your grandma can't take care of you, but at least you'd be close to her," he went on. "You could still do stuff with her like… I don't know, watch a movie? Grandmas like stuff like that, at least mine does. And she'll bake cookies for you, I'll bet. My grandma's cookie jar is never empty. And you gotta know that if you run off, they'll catch you, put you in another foster home somewhere. You'd have to start at another new school, right? You want that?"

"No." Dustin looked up. "I don't want to change schools again, but they put me in that math class with the high school kids. Those guys hate me."

"They're jealous. You understood that stuff Mr. G was teaching today, your first day in class. No one else did, including me."

"What?"

Jay sighed. Might as well admit it, he thought. "That class is full of freshmen, Dustin. I'm a senior. I'm in that class because I didn't pass it the first time, and I've got to pass it so I can graduate. I don't like it and I don't want to be there, but I gotta do it. At least you know what Mr. G is talking about. This is my second time in this class and I *still* don't know." He paused as a new thought occurred to him. "Hey, you know what? Maybe you could tutor me. I could pay you."

In the last few rays of sunlight, he saw Dustin's mouth fall open. "You want me to tutor you?"

"Sure. I bet other kids would, too. You could earn some money and then use it to do something nice for your grandma."

"I don't know." Dustin dragged out the last word. "I might be kinda busy working for Carly."

"Ah, come on, Dustin. You're just trying to hijack me for more money."

"Will it work?"

Jay crossed his arms over his chest. "No."

"Well, maybe I can."

"Yeah, and this way, you can show all the other kids how smart you are without being an annoying little butthead." Jay paused as something occurred to him. "Hey, I've been wondering about something. When you were sneaking into Carly's gardens and stealing stuff, how come we never saw any footprints?"

"I used a branch from a bush to wipe 'em out, then took the branch with me."

"I should have thought of that. So, now that we know you're smarter than me, how about that tutoring?"

From the darkness behind them, Carly spoke up. "I think that's a good idea, Dustin."

Jay turned his flashlight in that direction and she stepped out from the trees. Luke was right behind her. He hoped they'd heard all of what Dustin had said so he wouldn't have to repeat it.

Carly went on. "And I promise you won't have to move again, Dustin. You'll stay with me."

Luke chimed in. "Why don't we go back home and talk about it?"

Dustin hesitated. "Yeah, I guess we could. I'm hungry."

"Me, too. I'll bet Carly's got food," Jay said.

Carly laughed. "Since Dustin came into my life, I've always got *tons* of food."

Luke turned on his flashlight and put his hand on Dustin's shoulder, guiding him through the darkness. Dustin didn't shake off Luke's hand.

Carly stepped back so she could walk with Jay. She put her arm around his shoulder and gave him a squeeze.

"You're my hero, Jay Morton," she said quietly.

"Does that mean I get a raise?"

CARLY FINISHED PUTTING the last of the dishes into the dishwasher and turned it on. The house had been full until a few minutes ago. Now everyone was gone except Luke. Gemma and Nathan had come over as soon as she'd let them know Dustin was safe. Before Lisa made the trip to Carly's house, she had called Era, who was still upset over her slip of the tongue, but she'd calmed down now that she knew Dustin was home.

They had all eaten together and Dustin had been the center of attention, which he didn't like, but he'd been impressed that so many people had been out looking for him. Jay had quietly told Carly everything Dustin had said and she spent the evening trying to decide how she was going to handle it.

When she entered the living room, Luke was standing by the door, his keys in his hand, but then Dustin appeared in the hallway and stood staring at her. That meant he wanted to talk, although he wouldn't say so.

She told Luke she'd be right back and followed Dustin into his room.

"Ready for bed?" she asked.

He answered with his customary one-shoulder shrug.

Carly looked around the room. "We should repaint this room."

"Why?" he asked.

She suppressed a sigh. Did this kid have to question her on everything? It was probably all part of testing his boundaries. "It's your room and pink probably isn't your favorite color. You should have it be whatever color you want. Do you like blue? Green? Yellow? Red?"

"Orange."

"Seriously? Orange?"

His expression turned defiant. "You said whatever color I want."

She held up her hands. "Yes, I did. And if that's what you want, that's what you'll have, but why orange?"

Dustin shrugged again and looked away. "I just like it." He gave her a quick look out of the corner of his eye, so she waited until he said, "My dad had an orange helmet he wore to work. When I saw it on the hook by the door, I knew he was home even if I didn't see him yet."

Her throat clogged with sorrow for the little boy who would never see his dad's helmet hung by the back door again. It was a moment before she could say, "Then orange it is."

He moved toward the bed and sat. "How come you said I could stay with you when Grandma goes to live in that other place?"

"Sooner Community," she said, then chose her words carefully. "I want you to live with me because I care about you." She knew he wasn't ready to hear her say she loved him, although she did. "You've lived in enough places and need to stay in one. Like I said, this is your hometown now. It was your dad's."

He gave her a swift look. "Yeah. Yeah, it was." He climbed under the covers and pulled them up to his chin as he yawned. "Good night."

Carly went out and shut the door, then stood for a minute, composing herself before she went into the living room where Luke waited by the door.

"Everything okay?" he asked.

She nodded. "I think he was asleep as soon as his head hit the pillow." She reached up to rub her forehead. "I'm just so grateful he's okay. You should have seen his face when Era told him his mother didn't want him back, and then Era's face when she realized what she'd said."

"He ran away from her, didn't he? I didn't think he *wanted* to go back to his mom."

"He doesn't, but I'm sure he never thought she'd just give him away. I mean, who does that?" She repeated everything Jay had told her, including Dustin's mother saying that she wished she'd never had him.

"'An uncaring mother,'" Luke said, quoting Junior Fedder. He told her what Dustin had said about learning to play checkers from his dad and about his mother's boyfriends.

Carly shook her head. "That's terrible. Joe was a good guy. I'm sure he would never have wanted this to happen to his son."

Luke met her eyes. "So what happens now?"

"I'm going to adopt him."

He stared at her. "You're what? I thought you'd continue to be his foster mother."

Everything that had happened to Dustin, each interaction she'd had with him since the night he'd been caught stealing green beans, raced through her mind. The compassion, exasperation and affection she felt for him had been turning into love without her being fully aware of it. The idea had been growing in her mind ever since Era's announcement today. It was the perfect solution.

"I'm going to adopt him," she said, smiling. "He needs stability, love, a family, a mother who won't give him away when things get rough."

"Carly, you don't have any idea just how rough things *can* get."

"You're right. I have no idea, but I do know that if I don't do everything I can to help him, give him a secure life, it will be a tremendous waste of a valuable person, a brilliant mind. If I don't do everything I can to help him, I'll never forgive myself."

"Adopting him is a huge step. You'll be his mother forever. Do you really know anything about being a mother? After all—"

He stopped when Carly drew in a sharp breath. His face turned dark red. "I'm sorry, Carly. That didn't come out like I'd thought… well, I didn't think."

Carly shook her head. "Do you think I don't have doubts? I know it will be hard."

Luke considered her for a long moment before he said, "It's your decision, but…he'll be a handful."

"I already know that," she answered on a sigh. "But, think about it. Wouldn't it be better for him to learn to use his intelligence for good rather than for getting into trouble?

Besides, between the school counselors, resources from the state and his grandmother, I'll have help."

"You'll need help."

"I can do this, Luke. It'll be hard work, but I'm used to hard work."

"And you're used to tackling things on your own." He reached for the doorknob. "Good luck, Carly. Like I said, you'll need it."

"Thanks, I guess," she said. This was the right thing to do, but it wouldn't be easy. Still, excitement fluttered in her stomach at the idea of being a mom. "I'll talk to Era about it, and we'll tell him together. Then I'll call Child Services. I'm sure it's a lengthy process, so I might as well get started as soon as I can."

When Luke swung open the door, it began to rattle in its frame. The house shook and Carly looked down in time to see the hardwood slats lifting and moving in a wave across the floor.

Luke's arm shot out and he scooped her against him and into the comparatively sturdier protection of the door frame.

The quake built to a crescendo and then faded away. As soon as it stopped, Carly whirled away from him and dashed to Dustin's room, taking a relieved breath when she saw that he was okay and had slept through the whole thing. Luke was right behind her, peeking over her shoulder to check on the boy.

Back in the living room, she grabbed her jacket from the front closet and said, "I need to check the greenhouses. That was a big earthquake. I lose some panes or some plants every time we have one that's as big as that one."

"Can't it wait until daylight?"

"I'll stew over it all night. This is my livelihood and I've got to protect it, especially now that I'm going to have a son to raise."

"Then I'll come with you."

"That isn't necessary. I always do it myself."

He frowned in frustration. "But you don't have to. I'm here to help."

"For how long, Luke?" She looked up to meet his troubled brown eyes. "You'll be gone in a few months, and we'll still have earthquakes, maybe worse ones if your process forces wastewater back into the ground like the other fracking methods do."

"Carly, I wish I could guarantee that won't happen, but I don't know yet."

"I'm still wondering why you invested money in a process that hasn't been tested or proved."

Luke gave a little shrug. "I guess a person has to take a chance on something every now and then."

"Like I'm doing with Dustin."

"Touché," he said. "Good answer. So, now, take a big chance and let me help you check for earthquake damage."

"Okay, but remember I promised Dustin that he wouldn't have to move again. I can't keep that promise if my place is ruined."

"I know, Carly. Just a little while longer and I'll be able to answer all your questions."

Carly knew it was pointless to keep asking him, but her frustration was growing. He hadn't ever understood what a danger his process might be to her gardens. If he did, he would have told her exactly how it would work, what it would include and what the consequences would be.

She picked up two powerful flashlights she kept in an old painted and stenciled wooden toolbox on the porch beside the front door, and led the way to the greenhouses. She took one greenhouse and he took the other, and they each found a couple of broken panes and some toppled plants.

"Not as bad as it could have been," he said when they met by his truck. He handed her his flashlight.

"Not as bad as I'm afraid it's going to be," she added.

He had no response to that. Instead he said, "Aunt Frances tells me that the hospital finance committee—"

"Also known as Mrs. Sanderson's Arm-Twisting Society."

He grinned, obviously glad she was willing to lighten the mood. "Yeah. Anyway, they've got another fund-raiser, masquerading as a grand opening, in a couple of weeks. I was wondering if you and Dustin, of course, would go with me."

"You mean, like on a date?"

"Yes. Why not? You were planning to go, right?"

"Of course. It's Nate and Gemma's project,

and I've got a contract to provide fresh produce to the hospital kitchen."

"Congratulations," he said, smiling. "So, how about it? Will you go with me?"

"I don't know, Luke. I always go by myself to these things."

"Well, now you don't have to. You've got Dustin and you might need help riding herd on him."

"That's the truth." Still, she hesitated. "With everything that's happened since you came here, Luke, it makes it hard to—"

"Trust me?" He sighed. "Yeah, I know."

"I realize you're keeping a secret that's not yours to reveal, and I guess everyone has secrets of one kind or another." She pressed her palms together. "All right, I think one date to a public function, with a twelve-year-old chaperone, will be okay."

"Good. That's good. Thanks, Carly. Good night." His teeth flashed in a grin as he climbed into his truck and drove away.

Carly stared after him, thinking about the huge changes that had come her way today, and the ones still to come. Whatever happened with Luke, his project, her livelihood, she couldn't really affect the outcome. With Dustin, however, she could do something. She and Era could be a strong team, working together to raise him.

Luke's solemn warning that she was taking on too much caused her to pause and consider. The help he'd given her over the past few days had been valuable. It made her think about what things might have been like if their son had lived, if they'd raised him together, faced all his childhood issues together. It was a fantasy, one in which she couldn't afford to indulge. She had to remember that.

Hugging the flashlights, she ran up the stairs and into the house.

CHAPTER FIFTEEN

"I'VE NEVER SEEN a town as crazy about grand openings as this one is," Luke said as they stood on the lawn in front of the hospital and looked around at the crowd. A variety of booths had been set up. People could get healthy recipes, a blood pressure check or a foam-rubber sun visor with Reston Community Hospital printed on the front, along with the phone number. Other booths were signing people up to be hospital volunteers or organ donors.

"This is what passes for a glittering affair in Reston," Carly said. "And we love any excuse for a party, especially if Frances is involved." She pointed to the hospital entrance where Luke's aunt was greeting visitors. "Besides, the town, the whole county, was affected by the hospital closing, followed by the recession that meant lost jobs. This is like a resurrection of sorts for Reston."

She was proud to say that the husband of one of her best friends was responsible for this. Dr. Nathan Smith had returned to his hometown months ago to reopen the hospital his father had helped bankrupt.

The facility now had a full staff for the small emergency room, along with nurses, aides, techs, kitchen and custodial staff, and a trustworthy hospital administrator. Two more doctors had moved into the area and were on call along with Nathan. One way or another, dozens of new jobs had been created and the lives of everyone in the county were being improved.

"Carly, can I go find Jay?" Dustin asked. "He said I could hang with him and his friends."

She looked down and smiled at him. "Sure. They'll be selling food pretty soon."

Dustin pointed to the healthy food options booth. "Hot dogs made out of tofu?" he asked. "No, thanks."

"They'll have things you'll like, trust me. Do you need some money?"

He wrinkled his nose. "Nah, I've got money.

If I run out, I'll raise the rates on my tutoring services."

"Dustin," she warned, drawing his name out.

With a laugh, he turned away, looking for Jay.

"That is an enterprising young man," Luke said.

"I know." Carly gave him a worried look. "You don't think he'll grow up to be a con artist, do you?"

Luke shook his head. "Time will tell."

She watched Dustin walk away as she murmured, "I'd better start saving up bail money."

Luke laughed. "So have you and Era talked to him about adoption?"

"Yes."

"How did he take it?"

Carly tilted her head from one side to the other. "He seems okay with it but not enthused. Maybe I'll grow on him. He's had so many upheavals in his life, he probably doesn't trust me." She shrugged. "And why should he? I'm another adult, after all. Era will be out of rehab and into her own place at Sooner Community in a couple of weeks."

"Will she need help moving her things from her old house? I can help."

"Yes, she will. Her new apartment is small, but it'll hold her most important things. She's given me a list. The new owner doesn't care about the house, only the gravel he can dig, so he said she can take as long as she needs to clear her things out."

Luke nodded then placed his hand at the small of her back to urge her forward. "Come on, let's get in line for the tour through the hospital."

As they waited, they visited with the people around them and received many curious looks from those who knew her. She had dressed up for the occasion, wearing her purple skirt and a cream-colored, peasant-style blouse along with her dancing boots.

She had stewed over what to wear and second-guessed her decision to come to this event as Luke's date. Lengthy talks with Lisa and Gemma had convinced her to give it a try. They reminded her once again that they had her back and that he'd kept his promise to be helpful with Dustin. Lisa pointed out that the construction of his drilling operation was providing some jobs in the area, and he was making an effort to be part of the community. Carly wasn't sure when they'd become his biggest boosters, but their encouragement eased some of her worries.

There was that drilling rig, though. From what she could see, it was now complete since the new natural gas engines had been installed. She could hear them running but couldn't smell them.

Something had happened that morning. She'd been in her orchard, picking apples, when she'd seen a group of workers by the drill, laughing and clapping each other on the back.

She would ask Luke about it later. He might even answer her this time.

Since the hospital was small, the tour didn't take long. They'd slowed only when they walked by the murals painted in every department by volunteers. Carly had been part of it, painting jolly animals in the nursery.

When their tour finished, they returned to the festivities in the parking lot and saw

Shelby dancing with one of the young men Carly had seen working on the drilling rig. She was laughing at something he said.

"Shelby looks happy," Carly commented.

"She is." Luke grinned and bounced onto his toes. "Our initial drilling is going well."

While she was happy for him, she felt a shiver of dread run up her spine.

"For a first run, it was outstanding. I wasn't there for the drilling because I was helping Shelby."

He was barely able to contain his excitement. "Preliminary trials look like her process will work."

Carly nodded, sorting through her mixed feelings. "Good. I'll have to congratulate her, but you don't know the full environmental impact yet?"

His smile faded but he reached down and took her hand as he studied her face. "No, but I promise it will be far less than what my father had planned. I know it's hard, but please trust me."

All the reasons not to ran through her mind, but looking into his face, seeing the yearning in his eyes, made her nod. "Okay."

Luke broke into a grin. "Thanks, Carly. Let's get some food before the dancing starts."

"You're planning to take me dancing?"

"That's right."

"You never wanted to dance before."

"Don't forget, I spent years in South America. Where I was, everybody danced. I can even do the tango. Badly, but I can do it."

"He cooks, does laundry, dances. Now I've seen everything."

"THIS IS SO much fun," Carly said, stopping to catch her breath and grabbing a bottle of water. She poured some into her hand and splashed it on her face to cool off. She lifted her hair off her neck. Unaccustomed to having it down, she hadn't realized how hot it could be.

"You only say that because you actually know how to line dance," Luke complained.

"I can't believe you grew up in Texas and never learned how to do this." She gestured toward the rows of dancers, stepping and turning in unison, a moving line of color. Instead of a live band, a sound system had been set up, along with a few floodlights. No one seemed to care that it was getting cold and that this was hardly an ideal dance floor. Everyone was having fun.

"I guess I just never hung out with the right people." He watched the dancers as he filled up on water, too, then leaned against a tree. "I think the tango is easier."

"Maybe you could teach me. Someday."

Luke gazed down at her, his lips tilting in a smile. "I'd like that." He paused as she met his eyes. "Carly, this has been a great day. Thanks for coming with me."

Carly answered with a smile of her own. In spite of their history, all that had gone on before, and his current project, she couldn't help the warm feelings that flooded through her. Somehow, all she could recall was the way he had helped her with Dustin, had rebuilt the fence between their properties and held her as he told her the death of their baby wasn't her fault. She had felt a part of her heart heal when he'd said that. The ache for her baby would never leave, but at least it was no longer a cutting pain.

She wanted to tell him that, to thank him

for understanding, but Dustin walked up right then. "Are we going home, Carly?" he asked.

"What's the matter, did they run out of food?"

"I guess. They said it was time to close down. There was an old guy over there who makes his own beef jerky. I tried some. It was pretty good. He said he'll show me how to do it if I want to learn."

"Do you want to learn?" Luke asked.

"Sure. If I learn to make it, I could sell it and—"

"Of course." Luke shook his head.

"Which old guy was it?" Carly asked.

Dustin pointed across the way. "That tall guy with the beard."

Carly laughed. "Reverend Smalley? He's not old. He's exactly my age."

"That's what I mean."

"Very funny. Go get in Luke's truck. I've got to find the basket I used to bring the apples for bobbing. Yvette Burleigh and Misty Summers were in charge of that, but they've probably long since taken their babies and gone home, so there's no telling where my basket is."

"Okay," Luke said. "As soon as you find it, we'll go say good-night to Frances and Tom and thank them for a great party."

"Hang on to your wallet or Frances will have it emptied," Carly advised.

"She already did."

Carly laughed and hurried away.

LUKE STARTED AFTER her but someone from the drill site stopped to talk. It was fifteen minutes before he was able to get away and look for Carly. He found her in a hospital office with Gemma. They were looking through boxes and baskets for the one she had brought.

"Do you mean that old red-and-green one with the plaid lining? One time we wanted to fill it with stray puppies and set it in front of the supermarket to convince people they needed a new pet for Christmas," Gemma was saying as he stepped through the door.

"That's right," Carly answered, smiling in fond remembrance. "Although I removed the lining and ribbons."

"I was sure we could convince people to take the puppies. After all, we'd convinced the animal shelter director to let us try." Gemma sighed. "Too bad our mothers weren't in favor of the idea."

"Big disappointment that day." Carly glanced around. "Oh, hi, Luke. I'll be with you in a minute. I called Yvette and she said she's pretty sure she put it in… Oh, here it is." She pulled out the wicker basket and held it up. "Ordinarily, I wouldn't care, but this belonged to my grandmother. She used to gather her fruits and vegetables in it."

"I'm glad you found it. Is that all you need to take home with you?" He began urging her toward the door.

"Why, yes, it is," she said. "Are you in a hurry?"

"Not really, just thought you'd like to get Dustin home."

He glanced at Gemma, who swiftly gave him the watching-you sign, and he answered her with a grin.

They thanked Frances and Tom then hurried to the truck, where Dustin had eaten about three more sweet snacks, dropped the wrappers on the floor and fallen into a sugar-induced coma.

"How am I going to get him inside the

house?" Carly asked. "I could have carried him a few weeks ago but, thousands of dollars of groceries later, he's too heavy for me to lift, and I'm strong."

"It adds up, I'm sure. I'm amazed at how much this kid can eat. I'll help you get him in the house. It may take both of us."

As it turned out, they were able to get him up and walking into the house, though he was still mostly asleep.

Carly decided to let him sleep in his clothes and only slipped off his shoes and threw a blanket over him. If he woke in the night, he could brush his teeth and put on the loose T-shirt and smiley face–printed pajama bottoms he usually wore.

When she came out of Dustin's bedroom, Luke was sitting on the sofa, leaning forward, his hands running over Wendolin's trunk. She sat opposite him.

"I'm glad this is here, Carly. It's what she wanted and—"

He was interrupted by a knock on the door. Carly excused herself and opened it to find Jay standing on the porch.

"Jay, what on earth are you doing here at

this time of night? I didn't hear your motorcycle."

"It's parked over by greenhouse number one. I'm sorry, Carly, but I thought you'd like to know. I was in town, at the hospital party, and I remembered I'd left a book in the greenhouse so I came back to get it. I was reading while I was watering today."

"You were reading?" She couldn't have been more surprised if he'd said he was hula dancing.

"Yeah, government test on Monday. I've gotta pass it."

Carly felt someone at her shoulder and glanced back to see that Luke had joined them.

"Government test. You were reading, and…?"

"When I came back just now, the water was dripping from the faucet. You know how that one by the door doesn't turn off unless you really twist it?"

"Yes, Jay, I know. Is this about a leaky faucet?"

"No, about the water. There's something wrong with the water. It dripped all over the floor, and it looks funny."

Carly studied Jay's face. "The water looks funny? Funny how?"

"Cloudy."

"Cloudy?" She stepped outside. "And you only noticed it now? You should have told me right away."

"I am," he insisted. "I found it before you got back home, about fifteen minutes ago, and I was trying to figure it out myself."

Carly nodded. She couldn't encourage him to be a self-starter and problem solver one day and then berate him for doing that very thing the next.

Realizing she'd hurt his feelings, she said, "It's okay. I'm grateful you tried to figure it out yourself." She hurried to the greenhouse and Jay trotted along with her.

Luke came, as well, calling Shelby on his cell phone as they went. Hanging up, he said, "Shelby is on her way home. Be here in a minute."

"Did you check the connections to make sure the well water hadn't become crossed with any water from Luke's operation?" Carly asked.

"Yeah, but how could it? It's well water."

"We have no idea what's going on underground."

"I guess."

Luke must have heard this exchange because he said, "We've barely started drilling, Carly, and we've actually stopped for now. I don't think it's because of our operation."

"But you don't *know* that," she said as she reached for the handle on the greenhouse door.

"I can be pretty sure," he said, holding the door open and then walking in right behind her. He looked at Jay. "We'll need to check the water lines. Can you get some flashlights?"

Jay glanced from Carly to Luke, sensing the tension between them. "Uh, sure. I'll be right back." He ran to the work shed.

Terrified that her worst fears were coming true, Carly gathered up her skirt and crouched beside the faucet, where she turned the water on to a trickle, checked to make sure the spray wouldn't get on her plants and took a sniff. It didn't smell bad, but the cloudy color was alarming and quite obvious on the beige tile floor.

Luke came down beside her, touched the

water and then sniffed. "My test kit is in the truck. I'll get it."

He hurried out the door as Shelby stepped inside.

"Can I help, Carly?"

Clenching her hands together, she stood. "I…I don't know. I can't think of anything except finding this problem and fixing it."

Jay came back with flashlights and Luke with the water test kit. Carly filled a bucket of water and handed it to Luke.

"This had better be harmless," she warned.

Luke answered with a steady look and poured some water into a glass jar. It was definitely murky.

"Look, Shelby," Luke called out, motioning her to the table. "Have you seen this before?"

Shelby started to shut the door, but it was stopped again when Dustin slipped inside.

"What's going on?" the boy asked.

Carly looked up. "I thought you were asleep."

"I had to go to the bathroom. Hey, why does the water in the toilet look funny?"

"Oh, no," she said, her horror growing. She scooted back to the table to see what was going on. Jay moved to stand beside Dustin and told him, in a few words, what had happened.

"Wow," Dustin said. "We could be poisoned."

"Don't be stupid," Jay ordered, then gave the younger boy a sharp look. "Did you drink any water when you got up?"

"Uh, no. I had some juice."

Relieved, Carly smiled at him and nodded a thank-you to Jay for thinking of that.

Shelby took the jar and peered at it carefully, turning it this way and that. She sniffed it and frowned.

"Methane," she said.

"You mean like cow farts?" Dustin asked, startling a laugh out of Shelby.

Jay cuffed him on the arm.

"Methane, like natural gas stirred up by oil fields and oil exploration, right?" Fighting panic, Carly looked from Shelby to Luke and back.

Luke tested the water and then nodded at Shelby. "You're right."

"I guess it's possible," Shelby admitted. "But we've barely started drilling."

"Still, some of your activities might—"

"No," Luke said firmly. "It's got to be something else." He took a flashlight from Jay and went outside, heading straight to the well.

Carly grabbed the other light and ran after him. Everyone else followed along, but Luke put his hands out to stop them.

"Stay back," he said. "I only want to check for leaks."

"Water leaks?" Carly asked in confusion before her eyes widened in horror. "You mean methane leaking from the water well?"

"Yes."

"It could blow *up*?"

"Not if it's vented correctly," Shelby said. "Luke, you need to call the engineers over here to take care of this."

"I will."

"But we need to find out how it got here from your drilling site and stop it," Carly said.

"We don't know that's what's caused this," Luke said.

"*I* know that's what caused this." Frantically she looked around at the fields she was readying for winter, at the greenhouses, shed and house.

"This will ruin me, Luke. My land contaminated, my livelihood gone. What will I do?"

"First of all, we'll find out what caused this, and then we'll fix it," he said.

"That's easy for you to say. It's not *your* world being ruined." She lifted a shaking hand to shove her hair back from her face.

"But I'm trying to keep yours from being ruined." Luke reached into his pocket for his cell phone. "I'll call the engineers and get them over here first thing in the morning to see what's going on." He glanced up as he located the number. "Shelby, can you help?"

"Of course." She gave Carly a sympathetic look. "You know you can't stay here tonight. We don't know how widespread this is yet."

Dustin was watching and listening, wide-eyed and anxious, probably afraid he was going to lose yet another home. If it was only her, Carly would have stayed, but she couldn't take a chance with his health or risk another asthma attack. Realizing she had to be calm, at least for his sake, she said, "I'll call Lisa. She'd love to have houseguests overnight."

Taking a deep breath, she gave Jay a shaky smile and said, "Thanks for alerting me to this, Jay. You'd better go on home."

"I know this isn't a good time to ask, but do you think that I could have—"

"Yes," she broke in, half-hysterical and throwing her hands up in surrender. "If Joslin Gardens survives this, you're getting a raise."

"Now you're talking," he said. "Good night." He ran to his motorcycle and roared off.

Carly put her hand on Dustin's shoulder. "Let's get our things together."

Shelby said, "I'll talk to you tomorrow, Carly. Try not to worry. It may be nothing serious." She headed for her car while Carly stared after her wondering how this could possibly be nothing serious.

Luke's phone rang and he turned away to answer it.

"Come on, Dustin," she said, putting her arm around his shoulder. He must have sensed how bad the situation was because he didn't pull away. "I'm going to have Lisa pick you up while I turn off the water to all the fields in case there's a leak. I'll be over to her house as soon as I can."

Dustin went to gather his things and Carly called Lisa, who said she would come over right away. She hung up and rushed to her room to change into work clothes and boots.

When Dustin was ready, she hurried him outside and down the front steps to wait for Lisa, who arrived within minutes, her tires spewing gravel as she fishtailed onto the driveway and sped to the house. They were gone in two minutes and Carly breathed a sigh of relief, grateful to have such a friend.

Luke strode up as she was switching on the yard lights in preparation for shutting off the water and checking for leaks.

"I'll help you with whatever you're—"

"No!" Carly raised both hands, palms out. "No. You asked me to trust you and look what's happened. You said Shelby's process would be less harmful, but it obviously isn't."

"Carly, I keep telling you, we don't know that."

"But *I* do, Luke." She balled her hand into a fist and clutched it to her stomach. "I know it in my gut. Everything I've worked for might be ruined. I should have tried harder to stop you, but instead I believed you when you said you'd do everything you could to prevent harm to my land."

"I have, Carly." He took a step forward but she backed away.

"Get off my property," she said through trembling lips.

He shook his head. "You need help."

"I don't need *your* help. You may own the mineral rights to my land, but it's still my land and I want you off of it. And…and don't come back."

Luke stared at her, his lips pressed together in frustration. "I'll go, but I'll have people over here tomorrow to find out about the methane." Before he climbed into his truck, he turned and fixed her with a cold stare. "This isn't over, Carly."

"Yes it is," she said, wiping tears from her eyes as he drove away. She whirled around to turn off the water, grab her things and leave her beloved gardens behind.

CHAPTER SIXTEEN

"Ms. Joslin, did you know there used to be a landfill in this area? Right behind that hill." The hard-hatted engineer pointed toward the east as he gestured for Carly to join him.

She had been hovering, not wanting to get in the way but unwilling to be out of sight of Shelby and the crew she'd brought to look for the source of the methane. They had maps and charts of a type she'd never seen before, which they'd spread out on the hood of a truck and studied.

After she had reached Lisa's house and they had discussed everything that had happened, Carly had spent the night being alternately panicked about the methane, furious at Luke for endangering her land and furious at herself for trusting him. Mostly, she felt hurt and betrayed.

She had only herself to blame. History and common sense should have been enough to warn her to keep him out of her life, but she'd foolishly ignored both.

"Miss, is that your land?" The engineer reclaimed her attention.

"No, it's a neighbor's." She threw her hands out in frustration as she asked, "How is it possible I didn't know about an old landfill?"

"Has this always been your family's land?" he asked as Shelby walked up to join them.

"No. We lived in town when I was growing up. My mom worked in the school cafeteria and my dad was a maintenance man. My parents bought it thirteen years ago from…Robert Sanderson." Saying his name made her stomach clench. "But he hadn't owned it very long."

"People probably forgot. Must have been closed up fifty years ago, or more."

"And that's where the methane is coming from?"

"We think so." The man took out his phone. "I've got the name of someone at the county offices who might be able to tell me about the landfill. He probably won't like having to talk to me on a Sunday, but that's tough." He moved away as he punched a number into the phone.

"The old landfill has to be the source," Shelby said, joining them. "We haven't drilled far enough to have caused this problem."

"But what about the extraction method you've developed? Luke says it works. Congratulations."

Shelby smiled. "Thank you. I know you've probably got mixed feelings about it."

"I do, but I know what it's like to work hard for something and succeed." Tears filled her eyes as she looked around at her gardens. Wiping them away, she gave a wobbly smile. "So *now* can you tell me about your process?"

"It was a variation on the extraction method using kerosene. At the same time, I was attempting to find a better way to clean up the wastewater so it wouldn't have to be buried so far down, and all indications are that it will work as hoped." Shelby's face shone with pride. "I was trying to find a greener method, and I may have done it."

The engineer returned, breaking into their conversation as he said, "There is a landfill, but it was sealed in clay when it was closed. That was unusual for the 1950s, but not unheard-of."

"What has caused this leak now, though? Disintegration of the clay?"

He and Shelby looked at each other. "Possibly, but more likely it's the earthquakes. There have been so many lately, it probably cracked the seal."

Carly's mind reeled as she tried to take this in. "And they'll probably continue."

"That's right." His face was grim.

"So, even if this leak is somehow fixed, it could happen again."

"Yes."

She put a shaking hand to her head. "I'm ruined."

"I hope not, Carly," Shelby said.

"I'll take my crew and see if we can follow this leak to its source, but I can just about guarantee where it's coming from." The engineer joined his men and they huddled together in discussion. "We'll begin making a plan to seal it off."

"It will take a few days to get them here, but Luke called me this morning and said, whatever the source of the methane, he'll have tanks of fresh water delivered and refilled every week. That will provide time for a permanent system to be installed."

"What? But that would cost hundreds of thousands of dollars."

"Probably. And a long-term solution will have to be found so that your water will remain clean and you can maintain your organic gardens. When I talked to Luke, he said that needs to be our main goal."

Carly frowned in confusion. She had been so mad at him she'd kicked him off her land. "Why would he do this?"

Shelby gave her a gentle smile. "Because he loves you, Carly. He never stopped loving you."

Stunned, Carly stared at her as Shelby went on. "He doesn't even realize it, but you're all he ever talks about. And I think you love him, too."

Carly went very still as heat washed into her face. "I…guess I do." That was why this situation hurt so much.

"Sounds like you have a lot to think about. I'm going to go join the engineers." Shelby reached out and squeezed Carly's arm before she started up the hill.

It had taken someone she barely knew to make her see the truth. Thinking back over the past several weeks, she realized her love for Luke had been growing each time she saw him, whenever he helped her with Dustin, it had become stronger. Being with him had been fun. She had relaxed with him like she usually only did with Gemma and Lisa.

She hadn't realized that he had become so important to her because she'd been so focused on work, on Dustin and on her worries about the possible damage to her land. He hadn't caused the damage, but it had happened, anyway. It was no one's fault, but she had blamed him. She hoped she would get the chance to apologize.

WATER TANKS CAPABLE of holding hundreds of gallons were delivered and positioned by her house and greenhouses. Since she had only minimal crops planted at this time of year, her water needs were greatly reduced. Still, she thought about every drop of water she used on her gardens, in her greenhouses and inside the house.

She was so profoundly grateful for what

Luke was doing that she wanted to thank him, but every time she started to phone, she hesitated. What would she say? "Sorry for accusing you of ruining my land?" That could still happen. The engineers had sealed the leak, but another one could occur.

Their complicated history was even more complicated now, especially since she had fallen in love with Luke again. She had told Shelby she would give him time, but it was hard to do.

Halloween, always a big holiday in Reston, came and went. Dustin opted for the traditional and dressed as a very realistic vampire for the middle school party and came home happy. Era moved into her new apartment in town and Dustin went to see her every day before coming to Upcycle to hang out, do his homework and tutor his fellow students. Carly let him use the back room for tutoring because then she would always know where he was. He seemed to be settling in and, though wary, was coming to accept the idea of being adopted by her. They hadn't heard a word from his mother.

She'd taken Dustin to Tulsa to meet his

new family. Her parents and brother had been cautiously happy for her—and happy to have another kid in the family—but were worried about her handling him by herself. She was a little concerned, too, but had assured them she could make it work. Since she rarely backed down from anything, they believed her.

They visited the hardware store and bought paint for his room. To Carly's vast relief, he decided one orange wall would be enough. The remaining three would be white.

With winter coming, she had less work in her gardens, but instead of filling the hours with projects for Upcycle, she played word games with Dustin, or read one of the books she'd been stacking up for years. Mostly, she thought about Luke, their marriage and their baby. Memories she'd shut away for years were taken out, examined and put to rest.

One Saturday morning she was finishing her chores while Dustin helped Jay outside when she heard a vehicle coming up her drive. Her heart bounced into her throat when she saw Luke's truck approaching.

Her thoughts flew back to the day last

spring when he'd arrived with Wendolin's hope chest. Everything in her life had changed since that day. She wanted to run out and greet him, but a cold wind had kicked up. She didn't want to fight it to say what she had to say.

She threw the door open as he crossed the porch and held it as he stepped inside.

"Hello, Luke. How…how are you?"

"Okay." He shoved his hands into his jacket pockets then took them out again. "I know you don't want me here but—"

"No, it's okay." Emotion clogged her throat as she closed the door. "I'm sorry for what I said. I was frantic—"

"And you felt that I'd lied to you."

"Yes, I know now that you didn't. Shelby made me understand the need for secrecy."

"I came by to let you know that Dad and Tom are pushing the state to clean up that old landfill. It'll take a while, but I think they'll succeed in the end."

"And, thanks to you, I'll have clean water until then."

"The trucked-in water is working okay, huh?"

"Yes. Thank you."

Carly gave him a tentative smile. "Would you like to sit down?"

Before he spoke, there was a knock on the door.

"That will be my dad." He glanced at her then away. "He called and said he needs to talk to both of us."

"Your dad?" Her brows drew together as she said, "What could he want to talk to us about?"

"He wouldn't say, but whatever it is, he came all the way from Dallas to say it."

After another moment's hesitation, she opened the door. Her former father-in-law stood on the doorstep, turning his cowboy hat around and around in his hands.

"Hello, Robert."

"Hello, Carly. Okay if I come in?"

"Yes, of course." As Robert stepped inside, she gave Luke a puzzled look, but he shrugged and shook his head. "Please sit down."

With a nod, he sat, hesitating before he set his hat on Wendolin's hope chest. "I'm glad you've got this," he said. "It was important to her."

Carly couldn't think of a response. She'd

never seen Robert this…humble. She and Luke took the two armchairs.

"Go ahead, Dad."

"I owe you both an apology," Robert said. "There's no excuse for the things I said and did when you two were married. When you lost the baby… You were at the lowest point of your lives and I…I was a monster. I was still reeling from Barbara's death and I was trying to keep Luke from going away, having a life of his own." He looked up and gave a self-deprecating twist of his lips. "I'm not good with change or with giving up control. When he met you and you married within weeks, before I even knew what was happening, I felt everything slipping away."

Tears formed in Carly's eyes. "You were horrible to me."

Robert's face flushed as he nodded. "Yes, I was."

"The last time we spoke…you—"

"Bribed you to go away."

"And you promised you'd never tell anyone, so what are you doing, Robert?" she asked, glancing at Luke. "Why are you doing this now?"

"Because I can't do it again. I can't cause more pain to you. To my only son. I'm tired of keeping this secret, trying to justify it to myself. It's been eating away at my guts ever since I did it. There's no justification. No excuse."

"Dad! You bribed Carly?" The profound shock in Luke's face and voice were painful to see and hear. "I don't understand what you mean."

"Money talks, son, and I thought it would speak to Carly."

Luke shook his head and held up one hand as his gaze swung to Carly's face. "Wait. What? You mean you *took* the bribe?"

Miserably, she nodded. "He held the note on this place. He said he'd foreclose on my mom and dad if I stayed and forgive the debt if I left. Robert and I agreed to never tell anyone. I called Lisa and Gemma and they came to get me."

Shocked and angry, Luke said, "That doesn't sound like a bribe. That sounds like coercion. Blackmail." His attention swung to Carly, his incredulous gaze searching her face. "And you…you left me while I was at *work*. I came home to an empty apartment and a note saying you couldn't stay, our marriage was a mistake. I know we didn't talk much after the baby died, and when we did, we fought, but I was trying to give you space, time to heal. I never thought you'd up and leave. I thought you had postpartum depression along with the grief—"

"I did. Severely. And I blamed you for not standing between your dad and me."

Luke's lips tightened. "That part is true, and I knew that hurt you, but obviously, I didn't know everything that was going on, did I?"

"No. I should have handled it better, but I was in a terrible state, so deep in despair, it was a year before I even saw the sun shining again."

Dustin appeared in the doorway from the kitchen. Carly nodded toward his room and he slipped out of sight.

Luke stood abruptly and took a few furious turns around the room. "You wouldn't talk to me. I drove up here, hung around, tried to see you, but your parents were very protective. So were Lisa and Gemma. I thought you hated me, blamed me for the baby's death."

"No. That wasn't it." She closed her eyes but tears seeped from beneath her lids. "I blamed myself for what happened with…with the baby. I felt guilty for taking the bribe from Robert, thought if I was stronger, I wouldn't have done it. I thought I wasn't good enough, that you could do better, find a wife who wouldn't cause your baby to die."

"I never thought that," Luke said. "I wanted you back, but when you filed for divorce, I knew it was hopeless."

"When I…found myself again, I wanted to talk to you, tell you how sorry I was, but Wendolin said you'd gone to South America on a construction project."

Luke threw his hands wide. "Well, you know what, Carly? It's the *darnedest* thing, but they actually have telephones in Chile and they work just fine between there and Oklahoma."

Carly closed her eyes, finding it impossible to form words.

"And you, Dad. I always knew you were tough, that you didn't like Carly for I-never-knew-what reason, but I had no idea the depths you could sink to. All these years, I've blamed myself, couldn't forgive myself, but you...you—"

"I know, son," Robert said, the words catching in his throat. "I know. I'm hoping that what you said a few weeks ago is true, that even if you don't forget, you can forgive. I hope someday you'll forgive me."

Luke shook his head. "I don't know, Dad."

"I understand. I know I try to control everything. That's why I kept the mineral rights to this land. It was only business at the time, but now it's hurt Carly...and you." He cleared his throat. "Carly is the real reason I put a nine-month deadline on your project, which was stupid of me. I didn't want you getting involved with her again."

"Well, that didn't work, did it, Dad?" Luke asked in bitter tones.

"No. If I'd given you a one-week deadline, it would have still happened. Some things are out of my control." Robert stood, picked up his hat and settled it on his head as he said, "I know it will take a while, but I hope you can forgive me. You, too, Carly. I was a selfish fool and I caused you profound hurt."

Her lips trembling, she gave a small nod, acknowledging his apology but not yet ready to forgive.

Before he left Robert pulled an envelope from his jacket pocket and handed it to her.

"What's this?"

"Your mineral rights. All yours, free and clear."

Her mouth dropped open. "Thank…thank you."

He closed the door behind him and she expected Luke to follow, but he walked across the room to the big windows that looked out onto her gardens. Crossing his arms, he dropped his chin onto his chest and brooded.

She put her hands to her stomach, trying to quell the old nervousness that flared up when she felt she'd failed at something. She had never wanted Luke to know about the bribe. She'd known he would be profoundly hurt and betrayed, but she'd thought she'd had no choice.

In truth, she'd had a choice, but she'd made

the wrong one. She had never stopped loving Luke, but she may have lost him. Again.

"Carly?" Dustin started toward her, paused when he saw that Luke was still there, but then walked across the room and stood facing her. His worried face was a mirror of her own. "That guy, Luke's dad, was he mean to you?"

At his sympathetic tone, yet more tears filled her eyes. "Yeah, but I was mean to Luke, too, so it's bad all the way around."

"And you had a baby? That died?"

"Yes, I did."

"That's bad. I'm sorry."

"Thank you, Dustin."

"Well, Carly, if I'm going to be your kid, don't you want to tell me stuff like that?"

Carly wanted to laugh. Somehow she'd forgotten she had a ready-made ally in her house. "I should have told you. You need to know everything about the family you're getting into, the mom you're getting."

"Yeah." He frowned. "But with that cow-fart gas, are...are we gonna have to move?"

"No. Whatever happens, this is our home and we're staying. I know people have disappointed you in the past, making promises they don't keep. I won't do that. We're not going anywhere. We're going to be a family. No matter what happens, we'll be together."

He studied her face for a second and then said, "Okay. Good."

Tentatively, she reached out to give him a hug. He returned it briefly before stepping away, ducking his head to hide his embarrassment.

"Oh, Dustin," Luke said before the boy retreated to his room. "If it matters, I'm not going anywhere, either."

Dustin looked from Carly to Luke then, with a fleeting smile, he left the room.

Carly stood very still, her gaze fixed on Luke's face. Her heartbeat kicked up. "What do you mean, Luke?"

"I'm getting out of the energy business. I resigned from Sanderson Enterprises."

"What? Why? Because of your dad?"

"Partly. I returned to work for him because I thought I could connect with him. Omi thought so, too, and I wanted to be near her because I knew her health was failing. I can't work for him anymore."

"What will you do?"

"Not sure yet." He paused. "Carly, I want you to know that I never meant to deceive you about the drilling or the extraction process."

"I know. I lashed out because I was terrified and I felt betrayed. And I'm so very sorry about the bribe. At the time, I felt I had no choice and I wasn't thinking clearly. I *couldn't* think clearly."

"Doing what you did must have nearly killed you. All these years, I've felt guilty, never forgiven myself for not being the kind of husband you needed me to be. I failed at the one thing that was most important to me."

Carly's lips trembled as she said, "And I wasn't the kind of wife you needed me to be."

"We were kids. Not ready for marriage, family, any of those things." His gaze fell on Wendolin's trunk. "You know, Omi tried to tell me that marriage and family were much harder than I thought they were."

"She told me that, too."

"I think it's time to listen to her."

"What?" Her heart pounded, nearly choking her as she watched Luke reach into his pocket and pull out a small box.

"You just told Dustin that we would be a family, no matter what. Can I be included in that?"

"I think so. Yes." If she was willing to work hard and fight for Dustin, then she could do the same for Luke.

"Can we try again?" His caramel-brown eyes, full of hope and sincerity, looked into hers. "I love you, Carly. In spite of everything, I never stopped. Will you marry me again?"

Her lips trembled as she answered. "Yes. Of course, I will. I never stopped loving you, either. I realized these past couple of weeks that I've been running from my love for you, from everything that happened between us, from my sad memories, but I don't have to do that anymore."

"No, and I'm ready to stop feeling guilty for everything that went wrong the first time around."

"We can start again."

He grinned and stepped into the hallway, where he called out, "Dustin, is it okay if I kiss your mom?"

Carly gave a startled laugh but Dustin

seemed to take the request seriously. She heard his bedroom door open.

"Yeah, go ahead, but are you two gonna be doing that a lot?"

"I hope so. Why? You planning to make me pay for kisses?"

"Nah, they're free." He shut his door again.

Luke swept her into his arms, settled his lips on hers and kissed her breathless. Joyful tremors raced through her.

She pulled away. "Was that an earthquake?"

"Nah, honey, that was just a kiss."

She wound her arms around his neck. "Can I have another one?"

"Sure. You heard our kid say they're free. We've got twelve years of them to make up for." He kissed her again and then flipped open the ring box. A solitary diamond winked at her. "You didn't have an engagement ring before because we were in too much of a hurry. This time, we're doing things right."

"It's perfect," she said as he slipped it onto her finger. "Thank you."

"If you don't like it, we can always exchange it."

"I love it. Why would I want to exchange it?"

"No reason except I want it to pass muster with the Stiletto Mafia."

"The *who*?"

He told her about his visit from Lisa and Gemma and she shook her head. "They never said a word about that."

"Trust me, they've been watching me."

Luke replaced her arms around his neck and then linked his hands at the back of her waist, swinging her gently from side to side.

As they moved, Carly saw a flicker out of the corner of her eye and turned her head suddenly.

"What is it?" he asked.

"Wendolin's statue," she said, pointing to the figure on the mantel. "I think she winked at us."

Luke kissed her again. "Omi approves." He held her away from him and smiled down at her. "So, you're okay with marrying a guy with no job?"

"That depends. How do you feel about gardening?"

He grinned. "I like what I've learned about it so far. I could make it my new career. I've changed careers before. We can expand now that there will be two of us."

"I'd like that."

His smile faded. "I wish I could guarantee we'll never have an issue with the oil extraction plant next door, or the earthquakes."

Carly shrugged. "There aren't any guarantees in life. But we've already been through so much I think we can handle whatever happens if we stick together."

"I agree."

EPILOGUE

"I LOVE THAT you and Luke decided on a Christmas wedding." Gemma sighed as she adjusted Carly's veil then tweaked the ivory satin skirt. "And using the lace from Luke's grandmother's wedding dress was inspired."

"Thank you." Carly smiled at her two best friends. "And thanks for everything you've done."

"You're very welcome. I love this, too," Lisa agreed. "I've always wanted an excuse to wear a red velvet dress with a sweeping train." She twirled so that the hem swept the floor.

"I love it, too, but getting married five days before Christmas while also making holiday preparations has been hard work."

Gemma laughed. "When have you ever shied away from hard work?"

"Well, never, but now that I have a partner, that might be a different story."

"Now that you have a distraction, you mean," Lisa teased.

"Do you two know he calls you the Stiletto Mafia?" Carly asked.

They broke into delighted smiles. "Then our work with you two is done," Lisa said.

Someone knocked at the door and Gemma called for them to come in.

Carly's dad poked his head around the door. "Are you ready, sweetheart? Everything seems to be good to go up front."

"Yes, Dad," Carly said. "I'm ready." She picked up her bouquet of red roses and hooked her hand in the crook of his elbow.

"Me first," Gemma said, sweeping ahead of them. Lisa followed right along.

Her dad looked down at her. "How did you decide who would be maid of honor?"

"Alphabetical order. I was Gemma's maid of honor."

He laughed. "So Lisa will never get to be a maid of honor."

"Don't worry, Dad. Maid of honor, or not, Lisa is *always* in charge."

Her dad grew quiet, but his eyes were full

of happiness. "I'm glad you're doing this, honey. It feels right this time."

"I know it is."

They stood together at the church door as "The Wedding March" began and the audience full of her family and friends rose to their feet.

She walked with her father toward the altar where Luke waited, handsome in a black suit and red tie. Beside him, Dustin adjusted the cummerbund that encircled his waist, then looked up and grinned.

Everything that had happened in the past several months flew through her mind, culminating in this moment when Luke took her hand. Side by side, they stepped forward to begin a new life together.

* * * * *

Also by Patricia Forsythe:
HER LONE COWBOY,
AT ODDS WITH THE MIDWIFE,
and watch for HIS TWIN BABY SURPRISE
in May 2017!

LARGER-PRINT BOOKS!

GET 2 FREE
LARGER-PRINT NOVELS
PLUS 2 FREE
MYSTERY GIFTS

Love Inspired®

Larger-print novels are now available...

YES! Please send me 2 FREE LARGER-PRINT Love Inspired® novels and my 2 FREE mystery gifts (gifts are worth about $10). After receiving them, if I don't wish to receive any more books, I can return the shipping statement marked "cancel." If I don't cancel, I will receive 6 brand-new novels every month and be billed just $5.49 per book in the U.S. or $5.99 per book in Canada. That's a savings of at least 19% off the cover price. It's quite a bargain! Shipping and handling is just 50¢ per book in the U.S. and 75¢ per book in Canada.* I understand that accepting the 2 free books and gifts places me under no obligation to buy anything. I can always return a shipment and cancel at any time. Even if I never buy another book, the two free books and gifts are mine to keep forever.

122/322 IDN GH6D

Name	(PLEASE PRINT)	

Address		Apt. #

City	State/Prov.	Zip/Postal Code

Signature (if under 18, a parent or guardian must sign)

Mail to the **Reader Service:**
IN U.S.A.: P.O. Box 1867, Buffalo, NY 14240-1867
IN CANADA: P.O. Box 609, Fort Erie, Ontario L2A 5X3

**Are you a current subscriber to Love Inspired® books
and want to receive the larger-print edition?
Call 1-800-873-8635 or visit www.ReaderService.com.**

* Terms and prices subject to change without notice. Prices do not include applicable taxes. Sales tax applicable in N.Y. Canadian residents will be charged applicable taxes. Offer not valid in Quebec. This offer is limited to one order per household. Not valid to current subscribers to Love Inspired Larger-Print books. All orders subject to credit approval. Credit or debit balances in a customer's account(s) may be offset by any other outstanding balance owed by or to the customer. Please allow 4 to 6 weeks for delivery. Offer available while quantities last.

Your Privacy—The Reader Service is committed to protecting your privacy. Our Privacy Policy is available online at www.ReaderService.com or upon request from the Reader Service.

We make a portion of our mailing list available to reputable third parties that offer products we believe may interest you. If you prefer that we not exchange your name with third parties, or if you wish to clarify or modify your communication preferences, please visit us at www.ReaderService.com/consumerchoice or write to us at Reader Service Preference Service, P.O. Box 9062, Buffalo, NY 14240-9062. Include your complete name and address.

LILP15

LARGER-PRINT BOOKS!

GET 2 FREE LARGER-PRINT NOVELS PLUS 2 FREE MYSTERY GIFTS

Love Inspired.

SUSPENSE

RIVETING INSPIRATIONAL ROMANCE

Larger-print novels are now available...

LARGER-PRINT BOOKS!
GET 2 FREE LARGER-PRINT NOVELS PLUS
2 FREE GIFTS!

HARLEQUIN

super romance

More Story...More Romance

HSRLP15

WESTERN WP PROMISES

YES! Please send me **The Western Promises Collection** in Larger Print. This collection begins with 3 FREE books and 2 FREE gifts (gifts valued at approx. $14.00 retail) in the first shipment, along with the other first 4 books from the collection! If I do not cancel, I will receive 8 monthly shipments until I have the entire 51-book Western Promises collection. I will receive 2 or 3 FREE books in each shipment and I will pay just $4.99 US/ $5.89 CDN for each of the other four books in each shipment, plus $2.99 for shipping and handling per shipment. *If I decide to keep the entire collection, I'll have paid for only 32 books, because 19 books are FREE! I understand that accepting the 3 free books and gifts places me under no obligation to buy anything. I can always return a shipment and cancel at any time. My free books and gifts are mine to keep no matter what I decide.

272 HCN 3070 472 HCN 3070

Name	(PLEASE PRINT)	
Address		Apt. #
City	State/Prov.	Zip/Postal Code

Signature (if under 18, a parent or guardian must sign)

Mail to the **Reader Service:**
IN U.S.A.: P.O. Box 1867, Buffalo, NY 14240-1867
IN CANADA: P.O. Box 609, Fort Erie, Ontario L2A 5X3

* Terms and prices subject to change without notice. Prices do not include applicable taxes. Sales tax applicable in N.Y. Canadian residents will be charged applicable taxes. This offer is limited to one order per household. All orders subject to approval. Credit or debit balances in a customer's account(s) may be offset by any other outstanding balance owed by or to the customer. Please allow 4 to 6 weeks for delivery. Offer available while quantities last. Offer not available to Quebec residents.

Your Privacy—The Reader Service is committed to protecting your privacy. Our Privacy Policy is available online at www.ReaderService.com or upon request from the Reader Service.

We make a portion of our mailing list available to reputable third parties that offer products we believe may interest you. If you prefer that we not exchange your name with third parties, or if you wish to clarify or modify your communication preferences, please visit us at www.ReaderService.com/consumerschoice or write to us at Reader Service Preference Service, P.O. Box 9062, Buffalo, NY 14240-9062. Include your complete name and address.

WPBPA16R

READERSERVICE.COM

Manage your account online!

- Review your order history
- Manage your payments
- Update your address

> **We've designed the Reader Service website just for you.**

Enjoy all the features!

- Discover new series available to you, and read excerpts from any series.
- Respond to mailings and special monthly offers.
- Connect with favorite authors at the blog.
- Browse the Bonus Bucks catalog and online-only exculsives.
- Share your feedback.

Visit us at:

ReaderService.com